FACED WITH A
DANGEROUS CHOICE!

Your efforts to rescue the captured elven ruler Estragon have led you straight to fearsome Nightmare Castle. In the depths of the castle, you hide behind a pile of boxes and stare, aghast at what you see. A band of bloodthirsty trolls surrounds a terrified elven girl, who cowers in a corner. They're planning to eat her!

Nervously you finger your magical Jewel of Kaibak. If you have enough skill, the jewel will set the trolls to fighting among themselves. But if you fail to use it properly, your own brains will become hopelessly scrambled!

What will you do?

1) If you dare to use the Jewel of Kaibak, turn to page 135.

2) If you would rather sneak around the edge of the room in hope the trolls don't see you, turn to page 99.

Whichever choice you make, you are sure to find excitement as you lead the
RAID ON NIGHTMARE CASTLE

RAID ON
NIGHTMARE CASTLE

BY CATHERINE McGUIRE

A DUNGEONS & DRAGONS™ Adventure Book

Cover Art by Jeff Easley
Interior Art by Jim Holloway

TSR, Inc.
PRODUCTS OF YOUR IMAGINATION™

To Ken, for his love and support

Distributed to the book trade in the United States by Random House, Inc., and in Canada by Random House of Canada, Ltd.
Distributed in the United Kingdom by TSR (UK), Ltd.
Distributed to the toy and hobby trade by regional distributors.

DUNGEONS & DRAGONS, ENDLESS QUEST, and PICK A PATH TO ADVENTURE are trademarks owned by TSR, Inc.

D&D is a registered trademark owned by TSR, Inc.

First Printing: November, 1983
Printed in the United States of America
Library of Congress Catalog Card Number: 83-51041
ISBN: 0-88038-101-9

9 8 7 6 5 4 3 2 1

TSR, Inc.
P.O. Box 756
Lake Geneva, WI 53147

TSR (UK), Ltd.
The Mill, Rathmore Road
Cambridge, CB1 4AD
United Kingdom

ou are about to set off on an adventure in which YOU will meet many dangers—and face many decisions. YOUR choices will determine how the story turns out. So be careful . . . you must choose wisely!

Do not read this book from beginning to end! Instead, as you are faced with a decision, follow the instructions and keep turning to the pages where your choices lead you until you come to an end. At any point, YOUR choice could bring success—or disaster!

You can read RAID ON NIGHTMARE CASTLE many times, with many different results, so if you make an unwise choice, go back to the beginning and start again!

Good luck on YOUR adventure!

In this book, you are Kyol, a human orphan who has been raised by elves. Though you appreciate your step-parents' kindness, you long to have the chance to prove yourself. At this very minute, your thoughts are interrupted by the deep, echoing tones of the great gong in the village square. The gong can only mean that there is trouble brewing in the land. . . .

The great gong sounds, its deep tones reverberating in the village square. You drop your bow and hurry from archery class to the center of town. It's trouble or good tidings. Why else would the Elven Prince Novoye sound the gong?

Your friend Eddas stumbles into you in his hurry. "What do you think it is, Kyol?"

"I have no idea," you reply, "but I did see some travelers near the archery field."

"Oh, I saw them hours ago," Eddas says laughing. Then he sobers, seeing your hurt look. "I'm sorry, Kyol, but you know you can't see as well as we elves can."

"You don't have to rub it—" Your reply is cut short as the gong sounds again.

Rising fourteen feet high, the gong is of flawless clear crystal; it rests on a white marble base. The crystal is pentagon-shaped, faceted to send rainbows around the plaza.

The base is so highly polished that you can see every detail of your reflection. Your freckles and carrot-red hair stand out among the blond and white-haired elven folk of Cillisan. The slender limbs and thin features around you contrast sharply with your square jaw and broad chest.

Although strong, you lack the agility and speed of the elves, and you're reminded of this almost daily when Eddas, who is your age but a head taller, wins every race against you. As you glance over at the other thirteen-year-old, the crowd quiets suddenly, and the voice of Prince Novoye rings out across the plaza.

"My dear friends, we have had news from the North, from our kin in the Sotho Mountains. Great tragedy has befallen them: The evil warlord Rorlis of Gothraab has captured their ruler, our brother Estragon."

A gasp of horror rises from the elves, and Eddas says, in a choked whisper, "Estragon is the wisest among elves. He led the Great Council of Peace ten years ago."

You nod. You remember, as a child, seeing him briefly, and you recall the respect that he commanded. Even humans revere Estragon, whose reign has ensured harmony between elves and men for centuries.

"We have reason to believe that he is still alive," Novoye continues, and the elves sigh with relief. "Rorlis is demanding a huge ransom—money and elven weapons—for Estragon's release. We do not trust Rorlis to keep his promise to release our brother after we pay, and we have sworn never to let elven magic fall into evil hands. Therefore, we have decided to send our great hero, Canos, on a quest—to rescue Estragon and destroy the evil warlord forever."

"Come on!" Eddas says. "Let's see who's going with him!" You race off to the manor of the renowned Canos, Eddas's father. Although you've lived with them for almost seven years, you still haven't overcome your awe of the great elven magician. His stern manner and the exacting tasks he assigns make you nervous around him. He's a fair and a wise teacher, but you're never really sure of his approval.

At the entrance to the great hall, you stop. The tall, gray-haired Canos is listening to a stout elf with blond hair.

"Respectfully, I must point out that a large group will be quickly spotted," the stout elf is saying.

"True, Nyasa," Canos replies. "I will take only as many as needed."

"Oh, no!" Eddas gasps. "That means he'll never take us."

"The warlord Rorlis," Canos continues, "is an evil man but not stupid. He realizes the value of keeping Estragon alive and well. We should have time to get to the castle before—" Then he interrupts himself. "How was he captured?"

"He was traveling with his men through the Sotho Pass when Rorlis ambushed him. We think Salegarth the sorcerer was helping, and Estragon is no magician."

"That's very true," Canos says, then frowns. "No wonder Rorlis is able to do such mischief. Salegarth was powerful years ago, but I hadn't heard about him for a long time."

"Ever since he and Rorlis killed King Urlar, our ally, we've had nothing but trouble from that area—so much so that the place is now called Nightmare Castle," Nyasa complains. "The Prince would like you to win back the castle from Rorlis, if you can."

"I will make every effort, but rescuing Estragon is the first priority," Canos says. "It is a shame that Urlar died, and no one knows what happened to Queen Alesa."

Eddas races to his father, dragging you behind him. "Father, can we attend you on this quest?" he pants, sliding to a halt before the gray-cloaked Canos.

Staring down at the two of you, his clear, gray eyes thoughtful, the magician frowns. Nyasa, minister to the Prince, taps his foot, impatient at being interrupted.

You quiver! This quest is what you've been dreaming of! Finally, Canos speaks:

"Eddas, my son, despite your youth you have been of great service to me. It is customary for an elf to wait until one is at least fifty before going on an adventure. However, I will ask the Prince to grant an exception in your case."

"Huzzah!" Eddas skips around you.

"Do not make me regret my decision, son," Canos warns.

Eddas settles down immediately. "What about Kyol?" he asks, suddenly sober.

Canos glances at you and shakes his head gently. "It is but seven years since we saved him from the wreck of the *Noyal* in Antilia Harbor. Kyol's dying father gave him over to my care, and I cannot risk his life needlessly."

You sag in despair. Seven years might be nothing to the thousand-year-old Canos, but that's over half your life so far! Surely you can be as useful as Eddas! Feelings overcome your respectful silence.

"Great Canos, I know I am human, and limited, but I am still a cleric, and I've learned some of your magic besides."

Canos smiles kindly. "Your clerical training ended when you were six, and we have been able to teach you only a few simple spells. The amulet that your father passed on to you is powerful, to be sure, but you do not know all of its power. Your father was the great Dijbouti, a Patriarch known and respected by all, and you must give yourself time to follow in his footsteps.

With a wave, he dismisses you and turns back to the minister. "I will take only Eddas," he says, walking away, "and I will leave my assistant, Jadis, in charge."

That evening, bitter, you watch Eddas pack to leave. On his bed, he piles the clothes and maps he intends to take. He places his magic sword beside his pack on the bed, saying, "We had planned to draw our weapons together. I will sorely miss having you beside me."

"It's not fair!" you cry, holding your own elven staff tightly and blinking back tears. "My magic is as strong as yours and my arms are stronger, but I have to stay here with the children! It's not fair!"

Eddas slowly folds a cloak into his bag. "It's true that you are as good with your staff as I am with my sword. Perhaps Father is worried that you might forget your magic abilities during the crush of battle."

"But I've trained with my amulet until he was satisfied," you say angrily, "and I've practiced with the Jewel of Kaibak until I can set two dogs to fighting."

"Dogs are not orcs or goblins," Eddas replies,

putting his hand on your shoulder. You jerk away, still upset. "We are taking the jewel with us, but even I won't use it unless Canos is unable to. It's not called the Jewel of Confusion for nothing, you know. If either of us should make a mistake while using it, we would scramble our own brains instead of confusing our enemies. It can be used safely only in a calm state of mind, and which of us could be calm while risking such danger?"

You look sharply at Eddas. "And what about our training in intuition? Canos said last week that I was getting to be as good as you."

"Yes, he said that, for a human, you have superior intuition," Eddas agrees, "but you still can't hear or see as well as elves can; nor can you detect evil as well."

"Minor points," you mutter, sinking into a chair. "And I still think you need more than two elves to fight a whole castle."

Eddas stares at his feet, not wanting to make it worse by showing his excitement. "Would you like me to leave Graypaw behind?" he asks, nodding toward the sleek white whippet sleeping on the bed. At his name, the dog raises his head.

"Oh, no, you don't," Graypaw says firmly, in a voice Canos magically gave him. "I'm not giving up this chance at adventure to babysit some human."

Changing the subject quickly, you ask, "Isn't your father getting to old for adventures? His last quest was more than four hundred years ago."

Eddas shrugs. "When the Great Prince asks, you go. Besides, we're taking the jewel and my sword that glows whenever danger is near. We'll be well prepared to handle anything that tries to sneak up on us."

Your gloom deepening, you mumble, "I think I'd better get to bed. Have a good trip, Eddas, and come back a hero." Smiling weakly, you add, "Try not to get killed. That would destroy the powers in your sword, and why spoil a good sword?"

"Aren't you going to see us off tomorrow?" he asks.

You shake your head. "It would be too humiliating. I'll see you when you return." Realizing you may never see him again, you shake his hand quickly, and leave.

Entering your room, still absorbed in your struggle to accept Canos's decision, you absently greet your hawk, Tailspin. The hawk cocks his head, regarding you quizzically, then suddenly starts soaring around the room upside down—a trick that usually makes you laugh. You strain to concentrate on his antics and try hard to smile.

"Tailspin, I remember when you and I escaped from the *Noyal*. Your tail feathers were so badly singed that you couldn't fly straight."

"As I remember, you didn't look so good yourself," the hawk sniffs, settling, as always, on your shoulder. You smile, pleased as always that Canos also gave your pet the ability to speak.

Trying to relax, you reach for the sacred amu-

let. Holding it in both hands, you clear your mind. The deep-green jewel, carved in an owl's shape, glows with a warm light. You struggle to follow the path of the light to inner calm. Gradually the pains of the world subside, and only a gray fog swirls in your mind. After a moment, the image of a lone rider appears, moving through the fog that soon takes the shape of harsh gray mountains. In a flash of insight, you recognize yourself!

The vision disappears, and you open your eyes, smiling. "Why not?" you think. "I can follow them until they let me come with them." You will—you must!—disobey Canos . . . .

1) If you decide to follow Canos and Eddas, turn to page 117.

2) If you decide to obey Canos and stay home, turn to page 19.

It soon becomes obvious that the sounds of battle were farther away than you thought. Also, the unfamiliar territory forces you to move very cautiously into possible danger. By the time you finally reach the Pass of Laedris, only the remains of a great battle are to be seen.

Your heart beats rapidly within you as you begin searching among the bodies, weapons, and wreckage. To your great dismay, you discover Eddas's sword.

"It's my fault!" you cry. "If I had come sooner, Eddas would not be dead now."

"I don't think he is dead," Tailspin calls, wheeling slowly over the battlefield. "I don't see any elf bodies, and besides, the sword would lose all its powers if he were dead." Underneath all the dirt and blood, that blade glows, even though faintly!

"I forgot about the glow!" you say happily, then frown. "But that means Eddas is in danger! They're captive somewhere!" You pause, and a thought that has been nagging at the back of your mind suddenly surfaces. "How could one band of orcs defeat Canos? There must be evil magic involved somehow. And now that the trail has ended here, I have no idea where to find them."

"Think, Kyol!" the hawk says. "The orcs leave a trail of destruction wherever they go. It shouldn't be too hard to follow them. Just look for mutilated bushes, animal carcasses, good things like that!"

Sure enough! You find a trail and follow it for

three days, picking up clues as you go. You itch with the urge to gallop, but you must move slowly, or you might get off the trail and never find your friends. "The orcs," you think, despairingly, "know exactly where they're going!"

Knowing that a galloping horse can be heard miles away on this rocky ground, you keep the pace slow as you look for any more signs of your friends. That way, you hope, you seem just like an ordinary traveler on an ordinary journey. After another day of riding, Eddas's sword, tucked in your pack where you can see it, starts to glow brighter, signaling danger. So Eddas is still alive! And you're getting closer to the orc camp!

It's late afternoon when the hilly road drops suddenly into a gray, charred valley. You see smoke rising from a clump of dying trees. You see, too, that beyond the trees, the desolation ends.

"The orc camp must be among those trees," you say to Tailspin. "Look at the way Eddas's sword glows!"

"Perhaps the camp is underground, Master Kyol," the bird suggests.

Thick bushes line both sides of the road, providing good cover for any orcs that might be hiding there now. You're impatient to rescue Eddas and Canos, but that road seems the only sure way to the orc camp. You hesitate, undecided.

Then Tailspin sees a faint trail through the rocks. "Let's go that way," he says. "It's not wise just to walk up and knock at an orc door."

"But that way, I'll have to go on foot and it will take longer."

1) If you decide to take the main road to the orc camp, turn to page 114.

2) If you decide to take the trail through the boulders, turn to page 26.

Dawn is still an hour away when you wake and hurry out to your balcony. You could not find the nerve to disobey Canos's orders, so you stare in silence as the adventure begins without you.

The shadowy servants moving about in the courtyard are barely visible as they prepare the pack horses. Shields, staves, dried meat, and bread are piled high on the small gray ponies. Finally, the travelers appear and mount up. To avoid the warlord's attention, only Eddas will accompany his father.

Between the dark and your tears, you find it impossible to read the look on your friend's face. Gripping the railing in frustration, you watch as the caravan fades into the murky half-light. Sighing, you go inside to begin your chores.

A few days later, you see Jadis slumped despairingly over his supper. Left in charge by Canos, the elderly sorcerer has spent hours following the caravan by clairvoyance.

"What's wrong?" you ask.

"I can no longer see the Master's group. There was much confusion, and then nothing. I fear the worst."

"I knew I should have followed them! Maybe it's not too late."

You find out from Jadis where the group was last seen, and you ride out with Tailspin. You hope that you can still help your friends.

Please turn to page 117.

"I think the ladder will lead us out of this swamp," you say, starting to climb. You push through a trapdoor and climb up into a large room. At one end is a strange purple, balloon-shaped creature, with sharp claws on its hands and feet.

It bounces up to you and announces proudly, "I am the biggest Balagump in the world, and you're going to be my supper." Holding its breath, it puffs itself up to a round ball.

"What the heck is that?" Graypaw asks as Eddas pushes him through the trapdoor.

"Good! More supper!" cries the Balagump, grinning to reveal sharp teeth.

"I don't know, Graypaw, but I'm assuming it's dangerous," you reply.

Eddas and Canos push through the trapdoor and stand behind you, staring wide-eyed. At the sight of so many possible dinners, the monster chuckles in delight.

"Before I eat you," it growls, "admit I'm the biggest Balagump in the world."

"I'm too weak to put a spell on it," Canos whispers. "You're on your own."

Thinking quickly, you say, "Oh, I've seen bigger Balagumps."

"Impossible!" cries the beast, and it puffs itself up until it half fills the room. "Bigger than this?" it growls.

"Much bigger," you assure it.

Outraged, the beast takes a deep breath and pushes itself out even farther. You find yourself being pushed back against the wall.

"If it gets any bigger, it'll burst," you say to Eddas.

"Why not help it along?" he suggests, poking his sword into the Balagump's side.

You hear a gigantic POP! and the Balagump deflates instantly, until the body is lying on the floor.

Laughing, you look around the room and discover a door in the opposite wall. Yanking it open, you are astonished to see a distinguished-looking elf looking back at you. "Estragon?" you ask.

For answer, the elf looks behind you and cries, "Canos, my friend!" He rushes past you and embraces the magician.

"Good work, Master Kyol!" Tailspin crows.

"Now all we have to do is get out of here," you say.

"First we must rescue my daughter, Michelina, and my soldiers from the dungeon," Estragon tells you. "Rorlis reminds me daily of their suffering while I am treated well. He knows it is torture for me to have them suffer," he adds bitterly.

Estragon points out a magic portal in a closet. You notice the door in the far wall for the first time.

"Canos, can you unlock the portal?" Estragon asks. "You look rather tired."

"It's a simple spell," Eddas says cheerfully. "I could do that."

"Simple spell indeed," Canos replies. "Don't be overconfident."

Chastened, Eddas walks over to the closet, raises his hands as if to knock, and solemnly utters the spell. Suddenly, the walls of the closet disappear.

"Bravo, Eddas," you cry.

"Quick! There's no time to lose!" Estragon says. "We can go through two at a time."

You and Eddas go first. You pop out of the portal into a long, dimly lit hall, with many doors on each side. Each door has a barred window.

A few feet away from you, a heavy, black-bearded man is standing in front of a door, arguing with someone within.

"Uh-oh," Eddas whispers. "Something tells me he's not on our side."

As you slowly move closer, weapons drawn, the man looks up. "How did you get here?" he demands. "Who unlocked that portal?"

Tailspin and Graypaw suddenly pop through the portal. "Master Kyol, I do not like getting disembodied," Tailspin complains. Then he notices the dark-haired man. "Oh, no! Trouble ahead!" he says.

"Trouble is right, bird," the man cries, drawing his sword. "Whoever you are, I'll soon make an end of you."

"Rorlis!" Estragon cries as he emerges from the portal.

"I should have guessed they were your friends, elf," Rorlis sneers, moving toward a cell door.

"My daughter's in that cell!" Estragon cries. "Don't let him get to her!"

Immediately, you jump into action, swinging your staff at the warlord. Rorlis steps back, startled at the fury of your attack. Tailspin flies into his face, flapping his wings and momentarily blinding him. With a curse, Rorlis grabs the hawk around the throat.

"I'll finish you, you feathered nuisance—OW!" he cries, as Graypaw leaps for his arm, biting deep into the muscle. Rorlis releases the bird and struggles with Graypaw as you step closer. With a strong swing, you catch Rorlis on the head and knock him unconscious.

"Excellent!" Estragon cries. "I want to bring him to trial in my village."

"Nice going, Graypaw," Tailspin admits gruffly. "You . . . you saved my life."

"Well, somebody has to take care of you, featherhead," the dog says affectionately. "Are you sure you're all right?"

"I think he twisted my head around a bit," the bird says, settling on your staff and turning his head gingerly from side to side.

"Doesn't matter. Your head was never on straight, anyway." Graypaw laughs.

"Watch it, dog," Tailspin warns. "My gratitude only goes so far."

"Well, that's a relief," you laugh. "I thought for a moment that you were going to act like friends."

Graypaw sniffs arrogantly. "If you think that I'd associate with that animal—"

"Enough, you two," Canos interrupts. "We've got things to do."

You and Eddas tie Rorlis up with his own belt while Estragon frees his daughter. She rushes into his arms, crying, "Father, are you all right?"

"Perfectly fine, thanks to my brave friends," he replies.

They hurry down the corridor to free the other elves as you shake Rorlis awake and pull him to his feet.

With the warlord captured, Estragon's troops have little trouble subduing the castle. When the elves have rounded up the last of the enemy, Estragon turns to you and says, "I could use someone like you in my troops. Would you like to come to my village?"

"Oh, no," Canos says before you can speak, "we need him at home. Kyol's going to make a great cleric some day, and he's already a hero among his people."

You smile happily, proud to have won the respect of such friends.

THE END

"If Canos trusts me to save Estragon, then I can't ignore his wishes. I'll go, but only because he insists. I promise I'll be back to rescue you, Eddas, no matter what!" you say, gripping your friend's arm. You place the jewel securely in a bag hanging from your belt.

"I'll guide you out of here, but I'm staying with my master," Graypaw says.

"Who needs you? We'll find our own way out," Tailspin squawks at him.

"Quiet, both of you!" you snap.

With one last look at Eddas, you hurry back down the dark tunnel, holding a torch that you grab from a bracket. Suddenly, the tunnel branches into three parts. Which one leads to the outside?

"I can smell something strange in the left tunnel," Graypaw reports, "but also fresh air."

"There's light at the end of the right tunnel," Tailspin says.

"I think we came in through the middle tunnel, but I'm not sure," you tell them.

1) If you decide to take the left tunnel, turn to page 55.

2) If you elect to take the right tunnel, turn to page 58.

3) If you choose to take the middle tunnel, turn to page 42.

"I'd better sneak up on them," you say, starting up the trail.

The path is steep and you stumble often, cutting yourself. The sun casts long and frightening shadows. You glance back and forth uneasily as you scramble around the sharp rocks. The stench of burned plants makes your eyes water.

"By the time I get there, I'll be in no shape to rescue anyone," you mutter. Sunset leaves you in semidarkness, but with Tailspin scouting ahead, you find your way into a small cave behind some bushes.

"This may be the side entrance," Tailspin says. "All the guards are on the other side of the bushes at a bigger cave." The odor of horses tells you a stable is near.

As you creep quietly down the cave's tunnel, a faint light appears ahead of you.

"We're walking into a trap—I just know it," Tailspin grumbles.

"Shh! You'll alert every guard in the cave," you whisper.

"Tailspin? Master Kyol?" Graypaw's voice comes out of the darkness!

"Over here," you whisper, and the dog bounds up to you. Hugging him, you ask, "How did you get here? Where are Eddas and Canos?"

"I followed them," Graypaw says, "when the orcs took them captive. They're in the room down by that light. Mycrose is in back of all this, and he's working for Rorlis!"

"How do you know?" you ask, excited.

"I overheard them speaking as I hid in one or

another of the tunnels here," he replies. "Apparently, Mycrose has made several trips to Nightmare Castle."

"We'd better move fast," you say, "before Mycrose has time to do something awful."

Rough voices float toward you, and you realize the orcs are nearby. You can see the light clearly now, and it's coming from a half-open door at the end of the tunnel. On hands and knees, you creep the last few feet toward the door.

Inside, you see Eddas and Canos chained in an alcove. There is a white cloth around Canos's left arm, and you fear that he is injured. He seems to be asleep, and you hope he isn't under a spell. Curiosity overcomes fear, and you cautiously peer in.

Chains hang from the walls on all sides. You try to catch Eddas's eye, but he's watching a tall, thin man with dark eyes and a cruel mouth. Dressed in a black cloak and robe, he holds a twisted and carved wooden staff. His sharp eyes dart restlessly around the room, and you duck back for a moment. Two orcs, apparently guards, stare nervously at the chained elves.

"How can we keep them from casting a spell on us?" one asks in a squeaky voice.

"Fool!" the sorcerer growls, and the orc cowers. "The elves are secure as long as this lamp is still burning," he says, indicating a small, brass lamp smoldering on the table. "If it goes out, I'll have your heads on pikes tomorrow. I should skewer you, anyway, for injuring the old one.

The warlord at the castle won't be happy about this. If he complains, maybe I'll send you to him."

This must be Mycrose the Demon! So there is evil magic involved! And what was he saying about the warlord? Rorlis must want the elves to use as extra hostages in case something happens to Estragon.

Raising his staff, the sorcerer creates a flash of light, and the orcs jump. When the light fades, Mycrose is gone!

"Why can't he just leave through the door like the rest of us?" the larger orc grumbles.

"Relax. Sorcerers like to show off every now and then. Besides, guarding a lamp is easier than guarding magical elves." The two orcs turn their backs to the door and start talking and telling jokes.

Motioning to Graypaw and Tailspin to wait outside, you crawl into the room and hide behind a chest near the prisoners. Eddas sees you and smiles groggily. Canos looks up, but closes his eyes again quickly.

"If I wait, maybe I can sneak past the orcs and put out the lamp," you whisper to Eddas.

"Why don't you use the Jewel against Mycrose and the orcs?" Eddas says.

Unsure, you reach up and slip from the bag on Canos's belt a twisted gold armband containing a blood-red ruby surrounded by ice-blue gems.

This is the Jewel of Confusion. Properly used, it can cause one's enemies to turn and fight each other. But it also has the power scramble an unsure magic-user's brain! Both you and Eddas have trained with it, but Eddas is by far the better magic-user. Do you dare to use it?

A wave of fear hits you as you think of the consequences of making a mistake. You try desperately to be calm, but after a few minutes, you realize it's impossible. Blushing with shame, you mumble, "I can't. I'm too tense to use it."

"I understand," Eddas says. "I also would be too nervous to use it." You avoid his gaze, unable to appreciate his sympathy.

"Must . . . rescue . . . Estra—" Canos gasps. You both look at him as he struggles to overcome the spell. But he cannot, and his head drops onto his chest.

"Canos wants you to go ahead and rescue Estragon," Eddas whispers, nervously watching the orcs. "You must take the jewel and go."

Crouched behind the chest, you fight with your conscience. You don't want to leave your friends behind, and you're afraid you won't be able to rescue Estragon alone. But Canos wants you to go, and you don't like to disobey him. You shake your head in despair.

1) If you decide to take Eddas and Canos with you, turn to page 38.

2) If you decide to leave Eddas and Canos and try to rescue Estragon by yourself, turn to page 25.

"We traveled a long way just to help Canos and Eddas, and we're not going to risk failing them now!" you tell the hawk. Spurring your horse on, you race toward the sounds of battle.

It takes nearly an hour of hard galloping to reach the Pass of Laedris, where a small army of orcs have beset the party. From the side of the pass, more orcs are pouring through to reinforce their ranks.

With a yell, you ride into the battle. Swinging your staff fiercely, you finally reach Eddas, who is pinned against the rock wall by ten orcs.

"Hold on," you shout. "I'm right here!"

"Kyol!" your friend gasps, desperately striking at the wild horde around him. "Where did you come from?"

"We said we were going to raise our weapons together, didn't we?" you yell happily, but a new group of orcs keeps you from saying more.

You do your best to rescue Eddas, but more of the evil creatures push you away, and soon you also are surrounded. Feinting and blocking with your staff, you manage to avoid the roughest blows. You realize that the orcs are not fighting as fiercely as they could be, since several have missed easy chances to stab you. You wonder if they have orders not to kill you. But as you are knocked down, you decide that they want to give you a few good whacks, anyway.

Struggling to your feet, you see Canos off to your left. Blood is seeping from his left arm, and he is being held by two tall orcs carrying heavy wooden clubs.

"Canos, don't give up! I'll be right there!" you cry, but he gives no sign of hearing. Suddenly Graypaw leaps at one of the orc guards, snarling and biting. A swift blow with a thick club knocks the dog aside, and the orcs pull a strangely quiet Canos away.

Tailspin flies down into Canos's face, calling, "Wake up, great Canos!" but the elf shows no recognition.

A sharp knock on the head sends you down to the ground, dazed. By the time your vision clears, Eddas is surrendering. He drops his sword to the ground and raises his hands. Quick as a flash, Graypaw grabs the sword and runs off before the orcs can react. Screaming, a couple of them run after him.

"Run, Graypaw!" Eddas yells as the orcs roughly tie his hands against his sides. After a minute, the two orcs come back empty-handed. Graypaw has escaped! But you and your friends are prisoners.

The orcs make you stand up, and then they bind you tightly. They check you for valuables, but in their haste, they miss the amulet. They leave you the small bag on your belt, which only carries flint for making fires.

"We bring them in alive!" the orc leader warns. "You have your orders."

Cursing yourself for being of no use to your friends, you are led away with them. You notice the orcs have not taken the flint on the elves' belts either, and you hope the Jewel of Kaibak is safely hidden in Canos's bag. The only good news is that the orcs have left your staff behind, thinking it is an ordinary stick. Now, if only Tailspin will see it and pick it up.

You march over the rough road, pushed and poked by your sneering captors. Canos is up front, and Eddas is close behind you. Amidst the orcs' raucous laughter, Eddas's low tones go unnoticed, except by you.

"Canos was unable to speak or move his arms. There must be a powerful magician working with the orcs," Eddas tells you. "I'm afraid it might be the evil sorcerer Mycrose the Demon. He is supposed to be in the East, but I know of no other who could affect Canos this way. I fear all is lost."

"Maybe not," you whisper, trying desperately to think of some way to help your friends—and yourself!

For three days you are shoved and prodded along the road. The orcs are in a hurry, and you are harried mercilessly. They occasionally toss small bits of meat at you for meals, but you are afraid to eat it, not sure of whose flesh it is. The animals have disappeared, but Eddas whispers that he's sure he's seen Tailspin hovering not far away, and that he's holding your staff. Your relief at your friend's safety helps you to keep going.

The road crests the top of a hill and starts down, making the going a bit easier. Finally, you arrive at the orcs' stronghold, a cave hidden within a clump of trees. The horses are led to another cave not far away.

After stumbling along dark tunnels, you are untied and shoved into a small dungeon, but your captors drag Eddas and Canos away.

Alone and miserable, you stand in the middle of the dungeon, afraid to touch anything. The walls are slick with dripping water, and you can barely see your hand in front of your face. One of the orcs appears at the door, threatening you with a large ax. You struggle to appear calm, but you shiver in fear, waiting to be killed at any moment.

"Don't hurt him," the chief orc says, laughing. "Leave him here. He is of no use to us. But the elves are to be brought to the Master."

The sound of their footsteps fades down the tunnel. Separated from your friends, you sit down, not touching the walls, exhausted and hungry. Maybe Canos was right. Tailspin and Graypaw were more help than you were. You blink back tears as you try to think of some way to save your friends. As confused and depressed thoughts pour into your mind, you fall into an uneasy sleep.

Please turn to page 47.

"I think the road would be the faster way," you answer nervously, "and we do have to get out of here in a hurry."

You urge your horses along, as fast and as quietly as possible. Eddas strains his ears for any sound of danger. Canos is using all his strength just to stay on his horse at a fast trot. You ride alongside, watching him.

"I'll check for evil, if you wish," you tell him.

"Please do," he replies. As your horse moves smoothly beneath you, you clear your mind, as best you can, of your worries and fears. You concentrate on a spell that will let you detect evil close by. It seems all clear ahead.

"Tailspin, fly ahead and scout around," you order, and he soars away into the night.

A sickle moon appears over the top of the mountain to your right. Its light helps you to see the landscape. The boulders are smaller here and farther apart. You relax a bit as you see no sign of ambushers. It would be hard to hide any size army behind the small rocks and bushes that stretch out on both sides. You know you're more visible now, but you don't see anything to worry about.

"Everything looks peaceful," Eddas says, confirming your thoughts.

Suddenly Tailspin appears out of the darkness. "There's a camp farther down the road, and it sounds like a pack of orcs," he reports. You pull up the horses, dismayed.

"There may not be enough to bother us," you say unconvincingly.

"Do we want to take that chance?" Eddas asks.

"I think we should avoid them," Canos says, slumping in the saddle. "I don't feel strong enough to fight anyone tonight."

"I'll second that," Graypaw pants, sprawling on the road. "And you'll have to slow down if you want me to stay with you."

Tailspin settles on your shoulder and mutters, "What good are four legs if he can't use them when they're needed?" You shush him quickly, and after a moment's thought, you turn your horse to the left.

"I guess we'd better cut across the field after all," you say, leading the ponies off the road.

Please turn to page 50.

"Red dragons are fierce," you say. "I don't think we can handle it alone." You hurry back to Canos. "Canos, do you think you can manage a hold spell for a red dragon?" you ask anxiously.

"I—I think so," he replies in a low voice. He concentrates on the spell, murmuring strange words under his breath, while you keep an eye on the dragon.

Slowly, the dragon stops moving and gradually lowers its scarlet head onto its forefeet, snoring softly.

"Well, it looks as if it's held," you say.

Canos did so well that the dragon has frozen in place right in front of the inner entrance, completely blocking it! The only other ways into the castle are a nasty-looking tunnel and the ledge high over the stream.

The tunnel on the left is invisible from even a few feet away, its entrance tucked into the side of the castle's doorway. It looks just high enough to allow walking upright, and it looks as if it slants downward into the mountain. No telling what lurks in there!

"What do you think, Kyol?" Eddas asks.

1) If you decide to enter the tunnel, turn to page 62.

2) If you decide to try the ledge, turn to page 68.

"But Mycrose is gone for a while," you say. "If we're lucky, he won't be back before I have a chance to rescue you."

You settle down behind the large chest to wait for the guards to fall asleep. The cramped space makes your legs ache, but you're afraid to move them even a little. The hours pass incredibly slowly, and every time the guards stop speaking, you're sure they've noticed you.

Finally, when you don't think you can bear to sit still another minute and your eyelids are getting heavy, the guards start to snore. As quietly as you can, you sneak toward them. One orc is sprawled on the floor. The other has fallen forward in his seat; his head is just two inches from the little lamp.

Your skin is crawling with tension as you tiptoe forward. The guard on the floor grunts, and you freeze, terrified. But he just rolls over and starts to snore. Silently, you bend over and blow out the lamp.

Canos wakens as if from a deep sleep and smiles. "You have freed us, Kyol!" he says. With a wave of his hand, his and Eddas's chains fall away. The noise wakens the guards, but Canos freezes them with a word.

The three of you hurry out into the tunnel, and Eddas hugs a gleeful Graypaw.

"This way, Master Eddas," the dog says. "I know the way out."

"If he knows the way out, I'm a baby lamb," Tailspin mutters, settling on your shoulder.

"Shh," you say. "Let him lead."

Your party creeps along the tunnel, alert for orcs. Graypaw leads you quickly to the mouth of the cave. It's really dark now; the moon hasn't risen yet. Three guards are sitting on tree stumps in the bushes at the entrance. Quietly, Canos moves up behind them and murmurs a spell, waving his hands slightly. The guards suddenly stop talking and start to snore.

"That was quick," you say, stepping around them and moving outside.

"I fear my strength will not hold out long," Canos admits. "The wound in my arm needs a special spell, and being under Mycros so long has weakened me. I will need to rest soon."

"We can't rest here, of that I'm certain," you tell him.

Graypaw, following the scent of horses, leads Eddas to the stable, where he rounds up some for your journey.

"I've found one of the packhorses," he says, leading several horses back. "And it's still got most of the food and water." You wait impatiently for Canos to finish his healing spell. He passes his right hand over his left shoulder, murmuring the proper words.

"It is a shame you didn't find the horse carrying the magic potions, Eddas," he says. "They would have made the spell much stronger."

"No time to look for them now," you warn, mounting up. "We've got to put miles between us and the orcs."

Swiftly you gallop back along the road, with Graypaw racing behind you and Tailspin flying ahead, until you reach the crest of the hill. It's hard to see with only the light from the stars, but you stare around, looking for danger. A narrow road leads down the hill to a valley, in the general direction of the Sotho Mountains. The fields, too, offer a way to go, but you know the fields are strewn with boulders.

You wish you could wait until moonrise to plot your path, but you know that your group would then be too visible.

"It might be better to cut across the field," you suggest.

"The road would be faster, but it could be dangerous," Eddas says.

"You have done a good job so far, Kyol; what do you think?" Canos asks.

1) If you decide to cut across the field, turn to page 50.

2) If you decide to take the road, turn to page 35.

"The middle tunnel looks slightly familiar," you say. "Let's take it."

Creeping through puddles of stagnant water, you can hear your own breathing, and you hope no one else can. Graypaw slinks warily ahead of you, and Tailspin brings up the rear. Finally, you can feel a fresh breeze blowing in. "We're almost out," you whisper.

"Then you won't be needing me," Graypaw answers. "I'll be waiting with my master for your return, Kyol. Remember your promise."

"I'll be back as soon as I can get help," you reply. "You can count on that."

It's a clear night as you emerge from the cave's entrance. Telling Tailspin to look for your horse among the others, you creep quietly through the bushes concealing the cave. No guards are in sight, and you breathe a sigh of relief. Tailspin returns to say your horse is nearby, in a field right next to the cave.

"It looks as if it found the only patch of decent grass around here," Tailspin says. Moving quickly but quietly, you mount the horse.

You know the Sotho Mountains—and Nightmare Castle—are north of here, so you point your horse in that direction, using a special star as a guide. You ride across the field, and down into a valley, your heart racing as you wonder what lies ahead.

In the light of the crescent moon, you can see fairly well. The lush grass and the white meadow flowers are beautiful, but many patches of burned ground and withered foliage give evidence of the orcs' destructive passing. No animals or birds can be seen, and you suspect that they have fled or been killed. After a time, the desolate patches grow fewer, and you feel grateful to be even this far removed from danger from the orcs.

It's late evening of the second day before you see any signs of civilization. A small town appears in the distance, and you halt as Tailspin flies ahead to check it out. Tiny weathered cottages are scattered across the flat land between the mountains.

"What do you think?" you ask the hawk when he returns from his check. "Is it safe here?"

"It's far enough from the orcs, if that's what you mean," Tailspin replies. "I saw a church down the road; you might ask directions there. Maybe they'll have a place to stay, too. We could both use a rest," he says wearily.

"Good idea!" you say, spurring your horse on. You arrive at the little church at dusk, and a small, thin man appears at the door. His faded brown robe reveals him to be a practicing cleric, and his squinty eyes attest to long hours of reading.

The church itself seems to be in bad repair, with flaking whitewash and dirty windows. But the cleric doesn't look as if he has the strength to do heavy cleaning—or money to pay someone else to do it. You wonder what kind of guidance he can give this little town, but then you remember the orcs. "They probably keep him to warn them of danger," you whisper to Tailspin, who's now perched on your staff.

"I'm Alfrid," the cleric says. "Welcome to North Fork. Will you share my supper?"

You accept, eager for some hot food. After stabling your horse, he leads you through a long, one-story house, almost empty of furniture but full of dust.

A hall ends in a small, dark kitchen. Eyeing the pot on the dirty hearth doubtfully, you remove your cloak and ease yourself into a rickety chair in the corner. Tailspin perches on the top of the back door and promptly closes his eyes.

"What brings you to our little village?" Alfrid asks, watching you very intently.

Uncomfortable under his scrutiny, you say quickly, "We were just traveling in the mountains." You wonder why you don't tell him everything. It occurs to you that he might be able to help free your companions, but you keep silent.

"I've heard the mountains are dangerous," he says, still watching you. Shrugging, you nibble at the bread he offers. "Yes, some say it is a good idea to travel armed in the highlands," he continues, moving quickly to prepare a supper of stewed red meat and vegetables that you don't have the courage to refuse.

While eating, he encourages you to tell him more about your journey. You pick at the greasy food, eating as little as possible without appearing rude. Alfrid doesn't seem to notice. He explains that he doesn't get much news in this place. He does hang on your every word, you think, as you try to construct a story that doesn't tell too much.

After supper, the cleric excuses himself to lock up the church. "I'll find you someplace to sleep for the night when I return," he says.

The moment he is gone, Tailspin's eyes pop open. "Let's get out of here!"he says.

"Why? What's the matter?"

"Our friend isn't saying all he knows," the bird replies. "My bet is that we don't last through the night."

"Don't be ridiculous," you scoff. "He's just lonely for company. Besides, it's starting to rain."

"We have a better chance against the rain than against him," the hawk says. "Come on, Master Kyol—please?"

1) If you decide to sleep at the cleric's house, turn to page 56.

2) If you decide to leave, turn to page 70.

An odd, rustling sound snaps you awake. "This is no time to be sleeping," a familiar voice whispers.

"Tailspin! How did you find me?"

"He didn't. I sniffed you out. He'd have been lost without me." Graypaw's voice floats out of the darkness.

"Wait a minute! Who kept bumping into the walls?"

"Stop it, you two. This is no time for feuds. We've got to find a way to get me out of here."

"I stole the keys from the guard's table, and he didn't even see me," Graypaw says.

"Thank you. Now give me the keys."

"We also brought your staff. We figured you'd need it," Graypaw says. "By the way, it looks like Mycrose the Demon is behind all this trouble. As I waited at the entrance to the cave, I heard the orcs mention him."

"I supposed something like that was the case," you say. "Canos would never be overcome by a few orcs."

"Even more interesting," Graypaw says, "is that Mycrose seems to be in league with Rorlis. The orcs were talking about his trips to the big castle in the mountains, and that's got to be Nightmare Castle."

"Then we really have to get out of here fast," you say. "No telling what Mycrose intends to do with us."

Graypaw leads the way down the pitch-black tunnel. Now is your chance to show Canos that he needs you! Excitement churns in your stom-

ach as you search for an idea—any idea. But
since you have no notion of what to expect, nothing comes to mind.

After what seems forever, you reach a half-
open door and peer around it into a room well lit
with torches. Eddas and Canos are chained to
the wall in an alcove. Canos's left arm has been
bound with a white cloth. He looks as if he's
asleep, and Eddas is struggling to keep his eyes
open. That's more than mere exhaustion, you
decide. It must be a very strong spell that holds
them.

There is a door in the opposite wall of the
room, and through it you can hear orcs laughing
and talking. A small lamp burns on a table in
the big room, and chains of various sizes hang
empty on each wall. Silently, you creep into the
alcove, motioning the animals to stay behind.

"Kyol," Eddas whispers, "they'll be back
soon! You must get back to our village!"

Canos half wakens and shakes his head, his
eyes full of pain. "I don't think he agrees with
you," you tell Eddas.

Canos lowers his head and stares at his belt.
"I think he wants you to take the Jewel of
Kaibak," Eddas whispers. "Can you use it on
Mycrose?"

You slip the jewel from the bag on Canos's
belt. The ruby, bloodred, is set in a twisted gold
armband and surrounded by ice blue gems. The
beauty of it is quite deceptive—it is a powerful
magical item that, properly used, can cause
one's enemies to turn and fight one another. But

it can be very dangerous in the hand of a novice. Both you and Eddas have trained with it, but you are always a little afraid, and he is better than you. Do you dare to use it?

Eddas sees your conflict and says gently, "I, too, would be afraid to use the jewel. If you cannot, I will not blame you."

"Save . . . Estragon . . ." Canos gasps, fighting against the spell that saps his power. Eddas glances over at his father, then back at you.

"He wants you to rescue Estragon, and there's no time to lose," he says.

"But I can't leave you here!" you cry softly.

"You must," Eddas replies. "And you can't fight Mycrose with only your staff."

"But Graypaw says Mycrose is working with Rorlis," you say worriedly.

"Even more reason to go," Eddas gasps, his resistance to the spell weakening. "With us captured, Rorlis won't expect someone to try to rescue Estragon."

You look at the elf you have come to respect through the years since he rescued you, and you know that you can't do less than he expects of you.

Please turn to page 25.

"The fields will take longer to travel over, but the chance of meeting orcs is much smaller," you say. You ride for several hours, picking your way carefully over rough ground and sparse grass. The newly risen moon shines palely on your party as you pass from totally ruined fields to lusher scenery.

When you're sure the orcs aren't following, you halt and make camp, staying close to the small fire for warmth. Tailspin roosts in a nearby tree, and Graypaw sleeps with his head near the fire. Canos wearily rolls up in several blankets and instantly falls asleep.

Wanting him to rest, you and Eddas discuss the situation very quietly.

"You may be right about Father being too old for this trip," Eddas says. "I'm worried about his health."

"When I said that the night before you left home, I had no idea he'd have this much trouble this soon," you say, looking at the gray head half-hidden beneath the blankets. On this part of the journey, Canos has been struggling even to stay upright in the saddle.

Hiding your misgivings, you say, "I hope this rest will help, because we're going to need his magic at the castle."

"IF we get to the castle," Eddas replies. "Father's plan took us along a road east of here. How will we get there now?"

"According to the maps you brought, the Sotho Mountains are beyond this mountain range ahead. We're just farther west," you answer. "After we cross this range, we'll go east for a bit and then come up to the castle on the road you first planned to use."

"If we only stop to rest once every two days, we can be there in two weeks," he says. You agree, adding, "We can't allow much more time. Rorlis must get more impatient every day."

You discuss the rescue plans at some length. "Since we don't know what to expect, it's hard to decide anything concrete," you say, "but I'm in favor of sneaking in the back way, if we can."

"I agree," Eddas says. "The farther we get before anyone notices us, the better."

"Do you know anything about this sorcerer Salegarth?" you ask, poking the fire.

"My father said he once was a powerful wizard for good, protecting King Urlar and his queen. But something caused him to betray the king, enabling evil Rorlis to become the ruler of Nightmare Castle—and making Salegarth Rorlis's loyal servant. We must avoid Salegarth, if possible," says Eddas. "Canos may not be strong enough . . ."

You fall silent, contemplating the huge task before you, and then you sleep.

The next morning, Canos awakens refreshed and ready to ride. You explain the route you've worked out. "You haven't left a lot of time for rest," he comments.

"We don't know how long Rorlis will wait before he kills Estragon," you reply. "The longer we take to get there, the less time we'll have to rescue Estragon."

"That's true," Canos admits.

You're worried about Canos, but you hope hope some solution will present itself.

By the end of two weeks' travel through high, rock-strewn mountains, Canos is tired, but the castle looms in front of you. The entrance is shaped like a human skull, with an open mouth for the door. There are small windows dotting the front wall, and a tower soars up many feet at either end. The sheer black walls of the castle gleam in the noon sun and blend into the mountain cliffs.

No guards are visible, but you're sure they're somewhere nearby. A small meadow on the left of the castle has several horses in evidence, but no people. Except for a drawbridge over a fast-moving stream, there seems to be no way into the castle.

"So much for sneaking in the back door," Tailspin grumbles, perching on your staff.

Your party approaches the drawbridge cautiously. "There's got to be someone guarding the bridge," you say.

"Or someTHING," Eddas adds. "Shall we try the bridge or risk fording the stream underneath it?"

Canos says wearily, "If there's only one way in, then that's the way we must take."

Your eyes have been searching the castle door, the windows, and suddenly you have it! "Listen, Eddas, Canos! If we ford the stream, we might be able to climb in that window to the right!"

Your friends look where you are pointing. A small window sits several feet above the bank of the stream, to the right of the drawbridge. There is a ledge under it, which is accessible only by way of the castle door.

"I don't know," Eddas says doubtfully. "How would we get up there?"

"I'm no good at climbing walls," Graypaw complains, sitting near Eddas.

"It still seems better than walking right up to the front door," you reply.

Canos sighs and shifts uneasily on his horse. "Since I am so tired, I would not be much use right now against a strong enemy. Which route do you prefer, Kyol?" he asks.

You look from the bridge to the stream, then back. There must be a guard at the bridge, but you don't know how strong he might be. On the other hand, you're not sure your friends can get across the stream and climb up to the window. But you've got to make a decision.

1) You decide to try the bridge. Turn to page 79.

2) You decide to ford the stream. Turn to page 87.

"A little smell can't hurt us," you say, "and the air must mean we can get outside."

Waving the animals ahead of you, you tiptoe down the left tunnel. Soon you get a whiff of the strange smell—it reminds you of fungus and moldy wood.

"Whew!" you whisper. "I hope we don't run into a giant mushroom."

"Worse than that!" Graypaw yelps. "It's—" His voice is cut off suddenly. You move forward with the torch—and stare into the hairy face of a giant spider! Behind it, a huge web fills the tunnel. Graypaw, like an oversized fly, is struggling in the sticky strands. The spider quickly weaves a cocoon around Graypaw's body. Before you can believe your eyes, the spider has attached the white bundle that was Graypaw to the wall.

"He's right. It's worse," you moan. "Poor Graypaw." Saddened and angry, you thrust your flaming torch at the spider. Instantly, it whips a sticky white strand around the torch and pulls it from your grasp.

"Go for help!" you yell at Tailspin, striking at the spider with your staff. The spider leaps away, then darts around you, laying strands of web on your shoulders and arms. When you try to fight, the sticky fibers cling to your staff, and soon you too are wrapped in a thick, white blanket. As the spider attaches your cocoon to the wall, you hope that Tailspin can find help quickly. Otherwise, this is . . .

THE END

"Tailspin, you're imagining things," you say. "I'm going to sleep here, where it's warm and dry."

In a few minutes, Alfrid returns through the back door and says, "I have a spare room for you and your hawk."

"No, thanks," Tailspin replies. "I sleep better outside." Quickly he flies through the open door and into the night.

"My hawk's a little eccentric," you apologize, following Alfrid out of the kitchen and into the hall. He opens the door on the left side and ushers you in.

"It's not much, but it's dry," he says. The only furniture is a small cot in the middle of the room.

"It's fine," you assure him. He leaves and returns quickly with a rough brown blanket. Accepting it, you undress and lie down, falling asleep gratefully.

That night, your dreams are filled with dark images of sputtering candles and the murmuring of spells. Alfrid's face fades in and out of your mind's eye, grinning wickedly. Shuddering, you pull the blanket over your head, but the images still invade your sleep.

As you awake at dawn, groggy and sore, the smell of old candles raises the hair on the back of your neck as you remember your nightmares.

Through blurry eyes, you can see the remains of a magic circle around your cot. Half-melted candles sit at the points of a chalk-drawn pentagram. Each of the five points of the pentagram has a different magic symbol, to draw power from the four elements and the source of evil. The smudged chalk indicates that someone had walked repeatedly around the cot. Too late, you realize that Tailspin was right.

"Good morning." Alfrid grins at you from the door, and you groan. "I expect you'll want breakfast." His grin fades, "Well, you can have it after you finish cleaning out the stable. Now, get up and get dressed."

His words pull at your muscles, and you stand up to obey him. Strong magic has its grip on you, and you know that you have little chance of fighting it. Helpless to resist the evil cleric, you stumble outside toward the stable. He's made you his slave, and you don't know the magic to break the spell.

You do know that the spell will wear off quicker because of your hidden amulet. When you are free, it will be the time to see who is the master!

THE END

"A light means it's not far to the outside,"
you say, "if it's daylight. I've lost track of time.
Let's try the tunnel on the right."

You edge toward the light, hoping your boots
crunching on gravel can't be heard by anyone.
Graypaw and Tailspin stay behind you. The tunnel is not long, and the light gets brighter as you
near the end.

The light is coming from underneath a door.
You hear the murmur of many voices. Holding
your breath, you ease the door open and peer in.

It is a large room, lit with many torches and
full of orcs. Many are sitting, but some are walking around, talking and arguing. Finally one orc
leaps onto a table and motions for silence. "Listen, you bums—" he begins.

You shut the door quickly and hurry back the
way you came. This is not the right tunnel!

Go back to page 25 and choose again.

"It's probably less effort to walk around the back," you say, "and we might find some other windows lower to the ground." You lead the way along the rocky bank of the stream to the rear of the castle.

But it's not all that easy. The castle is enormous, and for what seems like forever, you follow a blank stone wall that twists and turns toward the rear of the castle.

"Are you sure this is a good way to get in?" Graypaw complains. "My paws are being shredded by these rocks."

"Perhaps you should get a better mode of transportation," Tailspin calls down to him.

"Tailspin! Haven't you anything better to do than torment that dog?" you ask.

"Certainly," he replies. "But nothing more fun."

Two hours later, you've almost decided to turn back, when a wall of thorn bushes blocks your way.

"Now what?" Eddas complains. "It looks like a dead end to me."

"Maybe not," Canos speaks up, stepping forward. Raising his hands, he quickly says the magic words that part the bushes. Leading the way, you enter a lovely garden.

All around you, acres of red, yellow, and orange flowers blossom among tall, white statues. The statues are carved of stone and depict warriors of all kinds, some with swords, some with clubs or spears.

Eddas pulls at your sleeve as a woman

approaches, riding on a magnificent white horse. As she nears, you see that she wears a white tunic cinched at the waist with a belt of gold, and collared with gleaming sapphires. And the horse she's riding has a single spiral horn rising from its forehead!

"Is th-that a unicorn you're riding?" you stammer.

"Of course!" she replies. "Now, state your business quickly."

Her proud and imperious attitude suggests that she's not a person to be trifled with. But is she a person to be trusted? You and your friends discuss her in whispers.

"She doesn't look like a monster, but you never know," Graypaw says.

"She could be a prisoner here, just as Estragon is," Canos suggests.

"She certainly doesn't act like one," Tailspin says, with a slight sniff.

"If we don't tell her what she wants to know, she may get angry," Eddas whispers, "and we don't know what powers she has."

You look at her, undecided. Her beauty makes you want to trust her, but . . . How could anything in this awful place be good?

1) If you decide to tell her the whole story of your presence in the castle, turn to page 129.

2) If you decide not to trust and not to tell her, turn to page 151.

"Let's try the tunnel," you say. "If it leads to the dungeons, we might find Estragon."

The tunnel is dark and wet. Every sound echoes back to you loudly.

"At least there's no danger nearby, or my sword would glow," Eddas says softly.

"This darkness is making me nervous," Graypaw declares.

You feel your way along the tunnel. Canos creates a weak light for a few minutes, and you see several small tunnels leading off the main one. You note the strained look on the magician's face and say, "We'll just follow this main tunnel for a while. We won't need light."

You approach each opening leading to the smaller tunnels with caution. "These smaller tunnels make me nervous," you say. "Something might cut off our escape."

Suddenly, Graypaw yelps once and disappears. The rest of you freeze, listening intently. You can hear Graypaw, but because of the echoes, you don't know where he is.

"At least he's alive," Eddas whispers, holding his unglowing sword in front of him. "I don't know why the sword doesn't sense danger. It must be here. Father, do you think you can bar whatever evil lurks here?"

"I think so," Canos says wearily, "for a little while, at least." You hear his voice echo softly as he says an incantation.

When he's finished, you say, "All right, let's go—slowly."

Suddenly your foot touches nothing but air,

and you plummet into a hole. You fall several feet into soft mud, and you hear the others yell as they meet the same fate.

"Is everyone all right?" you ask.

"Fine," Eddas says, "if you like muck."

Canos groans as he gets to his feet. Eddas rushes over to help him.

Tailspin flies down through the hole and lands on your shoulder. "Phew!" he exclaims. "What did you land in? Whatever it is, it's been here too long! Leave it to Graypaw to find something like that."

"I hope you fly into something large and hungry," the dog retorts, trying to shake the goop off himself.

You look up but the hole you fell through has disappeared. "Tailspin, go see if there's another way out," you say.

There's only enough light to see vague shadows. The light seems to be coming from one side, but you can't see what the source is. All at once, you are aware of something sucking on your skin!

"Leeches!" you exclaim, your stomach turning at the very idea of them.

"At least they're not big monsters," Eddas says, picking the bloodsuckers off his arms and legs.

Fighting your horror, you quickly rip the leeches off your skin. Despite your wet and dirty clothes, no physical harm is done, but depression takes over as you realize you could be trapped in this loathsome bog you're in.

"Why did they rely on my judgment? It's all my fault if they never get out," you think miserably. You shake your head, deliberately pushing aside these useless thoughts.

"What now?" you ask. "We can't go back the way we came."

"There's a passageway over here," Tailspin says, returning from his scouting. "It looks like the only way out."

You follow the tunnel, occasionally pausing to pick leeches off. The muck and the light soon disappear, but the stench remains, and your head starts to throb.

"This smells worse than a wet dog," Tailspin complains, then squawks and flies off, with Graypaw in hot pursuit.

"Get back here!" Eddas calls after them. "Do you want to fall in another hole?"

The offenders return, obedient but still complaining about each other.

"What did I do to deserve this airborne featherbed?" Graypaw grumps, glaring up at the hawk.

Tailspin settles himself on your shoulder. "I suffer more by putting up with you, I assure—"
You grab him by the beak, cutting him off in mid-tirade. Graypaw chuckles but wisely remains silent.

You seem to have slogged forever when the tunnel ends abruptly at what seems to be a blank wall. "What now?" Graypaw asks, pacing around the group.

"I hear something over here," Eddas whispers, walking toward the side wall. You walk up to the blank wall and feel around. After a moment, you feel a wooden pole. Exploring further, you realize it's a ladder, leading up!

"I've found a door over here," Eddas calls softly. "And I can hear people talking."

"I've found a ladder," you tell him. "It might lead up to the main castle."

"Or to another tunnel," Tailspin mutters.

"What do you think, Canos?" you ask. You grow nervous when there's no response. "Canos?" you whisper, moving away from the ladder.

"He's reciting a healing spell," Eddas says. "I think he was hurt by the fall."

"I'm all right." Canos's voice comes through the darkness. "But I am shaken up a bit. Have you found the way for us to go?"

You hesitate, not knowing whether to open the door or climb the ladder.

"Hurry up, Master Kyol," Tailspin urges. "Something may sneak up on us in the darkness."

1) If you decide to open the door, turn to page 144.

2) If you decide to climb the ladder, turn to page 20.

"That halfling might know where Estragon is," you whisper, as you peer through the half-closed door, "and if he's as unhappy as Bormer was, he might tell us."

Waiting until the halfling enters, you slip behind him and close the door. He whirls around, frightened.

"Who are you?" he croaks hoarsely.

Motioning him to be quiet, you hold up a key. "A halfling who once worked here—his name's Bormer—gave this to me."

"I know him!" the halfling exclaims. "I'm glad to help any friend of his. My name is Sim, and I'm at your service."

"Do you know where the elf Estragon is?" you ask.

He shakes his head regretfully. Then he brightens. "But I do know that Master Rorlis keeps his most prized possession, a magic potion, in a tower on the castle's north side."

"What good is a magic potion?" you ask, disappointed.

"It must have some worth, or he wouldn't value it so highly," Sim replies. "Now you must leave, for the Master will be here any minute!"

Following his directions, you sneak down the hall, past several closed doors, then up two flights of tower steps. You pause at the landing to look around. The upstairs hall turns a corner ahead of you, and there's an unlocked door to your right, which you open cautiously. Several brooms stand in the small closet, but nothing else. "It must be around the corner," you say.

Tailspin flies ahead, calling back, "Looks like it's all clear—OOPS!" He scoots back to you, as loud barking echoes down the stairs. "There's a door all right, with a very large dog guarding it," he says.

"Sim forgot to mention him," you comment wryly.

"Probably some relative of that miserable Graypaw," the hawk grumbles. The barking stops, replaced by noisy sniffing.

"I don't know if I want the potion that much," you murmur. "Is he chained?"

"I didn't have time to look," Tailspin replies. "With our luck, that dog would have magical powers."

1) If you decide to try to get the potion, turn to page 142.

2) If you give up and look elsewhere for Estragon, turn to page 89.

"Who knows what may be lurking in the tunnel?" you say. "Let's try the ledge." You coil the ropes around your waist before going on. "It's just as well we didn't bring supplies with us. They'd just be in the way here."

Slowly, you inch forward on the narrow space, trying not to look down. Graypaw follows you, then Eddas helps Canos to scramble up onto the stone shelf. Tailspin darts between you and the window.

"Watch out, Kyol!" Eddas says as you stumble. Catching yourself, you thank him and resolve to be more careful. Your view of the castle from here is limited, but you can see the road you traveled and the mountains beyond. The noise of the rushing stream below warns you that this is no place to enjoy the view. Suddenly you realize how vulnerable your position is.

"I hope no one patrols this area," you mutter, "because we'd be easier to hit than a stone dragon."

Grateful that you're not afraid of heights, you edge closer to the open window.

"If someone looks out the window now, what should we say?" Eddas jokes, but his voice is shaky. Canos is concentrating too hard to say anything just now.

The trip seems to stretch on forever, but finally you're under the window ledge, which is still way above your heads.

Please turn to page 94.

"Perhaps you're right. He does seem a bit strange," you say to Tailspin. Reluctantly, you gather up your cloak.

You sneak out the back door, with the hawk close behind you, and retrieve your horse from the stable. Silently, you ride through the drizzle, looking for a dry place to sleep.

Most of the cottages are dark, and you hesitate to disturb the occupants, any of whom might be in league with Alfrid. When you are soaked to the skin, Tailspin points out a large gray barn set back from the road.

Tying your horse out of sight and grabbing your pack, you creep in and look around. The ground floor is swept clean, but a ladder leads to a large loft filled with hay.

Removing your wet clothing, you spread it out and pull some dry things from your pack. Tailspin flies up to a thick wooden beam above you and settles down to sleep. You fashion yourself a bed and are about to fade off, when a sneeze breaks the silence.

Grabbing your staff, you cry, "Who's there?" For a moment there is silence, then a small man emerges from the hay. Looking more closely, you see that he's a halfling. Reddish hair like yours sticks up all over his head, and he's dressed in long underwear.

He's trying to look fierce, but you know he's scared. His arm trembles as he grips a small dagger, and there's sweat on his face, even though it's a cool night.

"If you mean me harm, I will defend myself,"

he threatens, "but I only want to get a good night's sleep."

Believing him, you decide he's no danger to you and beckon him closer. "Who are you? Where are you from?" you ask gently.

With reluctance, he answers, "I'm Bormer. I come from ... a castle in the Sotho Mountains. I ran away."

"That's where I'm going!" you say.

"Are you crazy?" he cries. "You'll only get yourself killed!"

"I probably will," you admit, "but I have to do it, anyway." Briefly, you explain your quest.

"You must be careful of the warlord Rorlis," he cautions. "Although he himself is not a magician, he has the evil sorcerer Salegarth working for him."

You spend much of the night listening to Bormer. Tailspin listens sleepily from his perch on the beam as the halfling reveals some of the dangers within the castle, which he also calls Nightmare Castle. He explains a hidden doorway on the side of the castle, and gives you the key which he stole to escape. He cautions you that the sorcerer has a spell on the room Estragon is in, causing it to move around from time to time.

"Rorlis is taking great pains to make sure his hostage is not recaptured," he says. "The room can appear in any one of five empty rooms throughout the castle. I don't know which ones. It takes a lot of energy to move it, apparently, because Salegarth does it only once in a while."

"Is there any way I'll recognize it?"

"Only the hard way," he replies, "when you run into guards or booby-traps. It's always protected by one or the other."

"I'll remember that," you promise.

"Rorlis doesn't have a lot of guards," Bormer says, "but Salegarth has laid many traps for the unwary. Never rush into anything."

He continues to give you advice into the wee hours of the morning. The next day, tired but happy, you thank him and ride off.

Two weeks of hard riding later, you're in the shadow of the great Nightmare Castle. The sight sends chills up and down your spine. The entrance to the castle is shaped like an enormous skull, with an open mouth for the door. You shudder to think of walking through that mouth to get inside. Tailspin, perched before you on the horse's head, squawks, "I've seen all I need to. Let's go home."

"Shh!" you warn him softly. "I said I would try to rescue Estragon, and try I will!"

Reaching inside your shirt, you finger the bag holding your amulet, and you relax slightly. Feeling for the Jewel of Kaibak in the bag on your belt, you wonder if you'll ever find the courage to use it. Pushing the thought from your mind, you begin your search for Estragon.

The castle's black walls blend into the gray rock of the mountain, and the bridge leading to the main gate looks treacherous, especially after you discover that a large, red dragon guards the main door!

On your guard for the soldiers that Bormer

said might be around, you study the castle. Small windows dot the front wall, and a tower at the other end pokes into the clouds. A small field to the left holds several grazing horses. There seems to be no other entrance, but Bormer said there was a hidden side door, so you search the mountain cliff carefully. You finally discover a narrow ledge-like trail cut into the mountain, leading to the side of the castle. Following it, you reach a small wooden door.

"This must be the hidden entrance that Bormer described," you say.

"He forgot to mention how small it was," Tailspin replies.

You decide to leave all your supplies on the horse, figuring you won't be in the castle very long. But you bring your staff, the amulet, and the jewel. Using Bormer's key, you unlock the door and walk, stooping, through the four-foot-high tunnel, with Tailspin following. Soon the ceiling rises to six feet, high enough for you to stand.

"I guess we can assume that whatever uses this route is pretty harmless," you whisper.

"Oh, I don't know—a four-foot-wide snake could be rather nasty," Tailspin replies. You shudder at the thought.

The hall leads to a large room filled with books and old furniture. A large table fills the center of the room. A large slate fireplace has unburned wood stacked in it, but the lamps are empty. The only light comes from an open window to your right. Dust lies thick on everything.

"We won't find Estragon in here," you comment, heading for the door in the opposite wall. You step cautiously out into another hall, springing back inside the room when you see a halfing walking toward you. You half close the door and peek out, watching the halfling. He doesn't appear to have seen you.

You're not sure what to do. If you hide, you might miss a chance to get valuable information. But if you show yourself and the halfling alerts the guards, you'll be in deep trouble. The halfling is nearing your room. You have to make a decision—fast!

1) If you decide to hide in the room, turn to page 86.

2) If you prefer to talk to the halfling, turn to page 66.

"I think smoke will do the trick," you say, looking around for wood.

"You two guard the ends of the hall," Eddas tells the animals. They split up, Graypaw taking the corner and Tailspin moving to the window. Piling tables and chairs from the hall before the open door, Eddas builds a quick fire with his flint and a little kindling, and you waft the smoke toward the bees.

"I hope Rorlis doesn't have a good sense of smell," you say, watching the flames inch along a table leg.

There are no alarms from Tailspin and Graypaw, and the smoke builds up until you can barely see the door across the room.

One by one, the bees sink to the floor. When you're sure they're all senseless, you hurry across the bee-strewn room and into Estragon's chamber.

"What if we can't break the spell?" Eddas asks. "Can we carry him?"

"He's waking up," you answer.

When he opens his eyes and sees you, Estragon jumps from the bed. "What is the meaning of this?" he demands.

You explain quickly who you are. "Canos is nearby," you say, "so we should hurry."

Shutting the door on the bees, you call Graypaw and Tailspin and head for the room where Canos is waiting. He looks up from a large book, surprised, as you enter.

"Good work!" he exclaims. "How did you find him? Are you all right, Estragon?"

Estragon nods, and you tell Canos quickly about the bees. You've barely finished when the door opens and a tall but stooped old man strides in, dressed in long purple robes with silver magical symbols on it.

"Salegarth!" Estragon cries and looks around for a weapon. At the same time, Canos closes his eyes and raises both hands, reciting a spell. Salegarth immediately raises his hands in a counterspell. As the magic flows back and forth across the room, you grip your staff tightly, wishing you could help.

Nobody moves for a minute, then Canos seems to weaken, stepping backward as Salegarth takes a step forward. Desperately, you swing your staff and hit the evil sorcerer as hard as you can. Surprise, then anger, shows on Salegarth's face as he moves to throw a spell at you. But in the moment that he is distracted, Canos uses his last energies, throwing a strong spell at Salegarth, which abruptly turns him to stone.

"Quick thinking, Kyol," Eddas says when the shock passes. "But you almost got killed—or worse," he adds.

Canos calls you to his side and says, "You helped me greatly by distracting Salegarth. Thank you. Now you can help us all by using your amulet."

"My amulet?" you say, instinctively reaching for it under your shirt. "How?"

"I haven't taught you all its powers yet," Canos replies. "Right now I want you to use it to call Rorlis to us. I am too tired to do it myself."

Under Canos's guidance, you gaze into the green, owl-shaped amulet and look for Rorlis. "He's heavyset, with a black beard and dark green clothes," Estragon says softly.

Suddenly you can see him vaguely, and Canos says, "Concentate on making him come to this room. Use all your energy, but don't think about danger, or you might warn him."

You concentrate deeply, and in a few minutes Eddas whispers, "I can hear someone coming down the hall."

"If I may borrow your sword, Eddas," Estragon says, "I will deal with him myself."

Eddas hands him the sword, and Estragon waits beside the door for Rorlis to enter.

The doorknob turns and Rorlis steps inside. He freezes as he sees his sorcerer, turned to stone. Estragon quickly holds the sword to the warlord's throat and says, "Now you're the hostage, O mighty warlord." Outnumbered and without his sorcerer, Rorlis screams with rage as he realizes that he must surrender.

"Now we must rescue my daughter and troops from the dungeons," Estragon says.

"Do you know the way?" you ask, watching Canos anxiously as he sinks into a chair.

"I think so," Estragon says. "But we can force Rorlis to show us the way."

You look over at the very tired Canos. "Do you want to wait here?" you ask him. "There is little danger now."

"I'll stay with him," Eddas replies. "In case any guards wander in."

Tailspin follows you, Estragon, and Rorlis down the hall. At the far end, the elf turns left to a stone staircase descending into darkness. At the bottom, a dimly lit row of dungeon cells extends in both directions.

"Michelina?" Estragon calls out.

"Here, Father." Her reply comes from far down the hall. You both hurry to her, passing a narrow wooden staircase on the way.

Estragon frees his daughter quickly, and she rushes into his arms. You keep an eye on Rorlis as you watch the joyful reunion.

She tells him, "The rest of the elves are at the other end of the dungeon."

When you reach the other end, Estragon releases his elves and says, "Since we have Rorlis captive, all we need to do is round up his troops."

The elves spread out, combing the castle for Rorlis's men. When the enemy finds out that Rorlis is captured, they offer no resistance, and soon most are in the dungeon.

Leaving Estragon and his elves in charge of the castle, your party returns to your Cillisan, and Canos says Prince Novoye will make you an official, perhaps a liaison between the elves and men. You smile, knowing your adventures are just beginning.

THE END

"We might find it impossible to ford the stream," you say, "but at least we KNOW there's an entrance past the bridge."

You leave your horses and supplies—except for several lengths of rope—near the meadow and proceed on foot, with weapons in hand.

"I hope whatever is guarding the door doesn't eat dogs," Graypaw says, padding soundlessly next to Eddas.

Tailspin, sitting on your shoulder, comments, "The way our luck has been running, it will eat anything and everything!"

You chuckle. "I don't intend to let it eat me," you assure him. "The only thing I intend is to tie up Rorlis with these lengths of rope," you joke.

Canos laughs. "I just hope you have the opportunity, Kyol," he says.

You and the others move up to the draw-bridge, with you intently watching the front door, while Eddas keeps his eyes out for hidden guards. Halfway across the wooden planks, you stop abruptly, your eyes wide. Canos comes up behind you. "What's wrong?" he asks you.

"Am I imagining things, or is that a gigantic nose sticking out of the door?" you ask nervously.

Edging forward cautiously, you discover the nose belongs to a very large, red dragon, a dragon that is watching you closely. Its large eyes, like fireballs, glare at you, and its sharp claws click menacingly on the slate tiles inside the door. It has made no move yet, and you motion to Eddas to come over.

"Do you think it's trying to decide whether or not to eat us?" you ask in a whisper.

"I'm not sure I want to stay until it makes up its mind," Eddas says hastily. "What do you think we should do?"

1) "I want to fight it!" If that is your choice, turn to page 93.

2) "Maybe we can talk to it." Turn to page 83.

3) "Maybe Canos can use a spell on it." Turn to page 37.

"If the dragon is trained to eat everyone who comes along, guests couldn't get in," you say.

"What makes you think this Rorlis gets visitors?" Eddas asks, scowling.

"Come on, let's find out," you reply. Politely yelling "Hello!", you move slowly up to the dragon. Its red skin gleams like a fiery sunset, and you notice a large silver chain around its leg. You ask permission to enter, saying you have friends in the castle.

"Which isn't a lie," Graypaw points out.

"I must tell the Master of this castle that you are here," the dragon rumbles, emitting breath that smells of brimstone. "What are your names?"

"We can't tell Rorlis we're here," Eddas whispers to you urgently. "That will spoil everything!"

"I'll try to stall him," you whisper back. Stepping a tiny bit closer, you say, "I noticed you're chained up. Would you escape if you could?"

"Of course," the dragon replies. "I was captured four years ago, and I haven't seen my family since then."

"I think we can set you free if you'll not warn anyone that we're here," you offer. Turning to Eddas, you ask softly, "Can you release that lock?"

"I think so," he replies, "as long as there's not a strong spell on it."

Walking as close to the dragon as he dares, Eddas stretches both hands out toward the lock. He closes his eyes and concentrates on the words of the spell. Suddenly the heavy chain falls away from the dragon's leg! Immediately, the dragon moves out onto the bridge. You watch it nervously, hoping it's the grateful kind.

"How can I ever thank you?" the dragon asks, smiling gratefully.

"Could you tell us where Estragon is hidden?" you ask in a small voice.

"I don't know that, because the sorcerer causes the room to move, to keep anyone from finding him. I'm not sure, but I think there are five positions that the room can be in, from the tower down to the lower floors. The room is always guarded or booby-trapped, wherever it is. That's all I know," it says. "Sorry."

"That's okay," you say quickly. "You'd better get away before they see you."

Gratefully, the dragon flies away, and you motion Canos and the animals to join you.

"That was quick thinking, Kyol," Canos says, smiling. "And you did that spell very smoothly," he tells his son.

Both of you grin and wave off the compliment. "It was nothing," you say, secretly very pleased at his approval.

Your grinning stops as you lead the way through the now-unguarded doors of Nightmare Castle. You have a strange feeling as you enter the open mouth of the skull that forms the doorway—as if the jaws were waiting for an opportunity to snap shut!

As you enter the castle, a wide hallway stretches in front of you. The ceiling is at least twelve feet high, and a rich burgundy carpet covers the floor. Torches sputter in brackets on both sides, and several doors are spaced along the wall.

"Well, this doesn't look too evil," Eddas says, surprised. Graypaw peers down the hall from behind his master's legs.

"In this case, what we don't know CAN hurt us," you reply, staring up the wide stone staircase to the left. The smooth, gray marble bannister curves gracefully toward the middle of the hall. A second glance reveals that the railings are carved to look like human skulls! At least, you hope they're carved—and not real.

"Which way, Kyol?" Eddas asks.

1) If you want to climb the stairs, turn to page 107.

2) If you want to walk straight down the hall, turn to page 110.

"Quick, Tailspin, let's hide!" you whisper, looking around the room. "That halfling may be harmless, but he might have a bigger friend nearby."

Looking around, you see few places to hide. The large table has a cloth on it, but you'd feel insecure kneeling underneath. Tailspin has flown to the mantelpiece and, with eyes closed, looks just like a black stone statue. "That's fine for you . . ." you mumble, desperately looking around.

You duck behind the curtain on the wall, but quickly realize your feet are showing. Panic seizes you, and for a moment you can't think. "Calm down," you murmur, leaning against the wall and trying to breathe normally. Suddenly you discover that you are leaning against a door.

"This could lead to something worse than the halfling," you murmur. "But on the other hand . . ."

1) If you decide to go through the door, turn to page 111.

2) If you decide to hide under the table, turn to page 105.

"The stream will be difficult, but at least we'll be out of sight," you say, leading the way down to the bank.

Since you are the stronger, you volunteer to swim over with ropes and fashion a safety device for the others. You tie one end of a rope to a bridge pylon. Carrying another rope, you dive into the icy stream, where you fight your way to the opposite bank. Dripping and cold, you tie the other end of the rope to another pylon.

"Tell them to be careful," you instruct Tailspin. "The current is strong!" The hawk flies over and relays your message quickly.

Canos wades in first, holding on to the stout rope. The water sweeps around and over him, and for a moment you think he's gone under. Eddas wades in right behind him. He holds the rope with one hand while reaching for his father with the other.

"I can almost stand," Eddas calls to you as they reach midstream. Graypaw hesitates, and Tailspin laughs raucously. Angrily, the dog plunges in and swims across behind the elves.

You grab Canos and help him ashore. Eddas staggers out, then reaches back for his unhappy dog. Graypaw stands dripping and miserable next to his master. Only Tailspin isn't soaked to the skin.

You look straight up at the castle wall. The window seems higher than it did from the road, but you see that it is open.

You look to your right and discover that there is a walkway between the castle and the stream, and it seems to go all the way around back.

"Shall we go around and look?" you ask the group. "Our only other choice is to climb up to that window."

Eddas looks up at the window doubtfully. "It's a long climb," he says.

Tailspin flies up to the window, then returns and sits on your shoulder. "The room is empty right now," he says.

Canos shivers a little in his wet clothes and says, "If the path to the back leads to a dead end, we could be trapped by guards."

"But we haven't seen any guards yet," you argue, "and walking is easier than climbing."

"I've tried to use my intuition to make a good choice, but I'm too tired," Eddas complains.

"Well, somebody make a choice soon," Graypaw says irritably. "I'm freezing just standing here."

"What about you, Kyol?" Canos asks. "What does your intuition tell you?"

1) If you decide to go in the window, turn to page 94.

2) If you decide to go around the back, turn to page 59.

"We've come here to find Estragon, not a magic potion," you tell Tailspin. "Come on."

Returning down the stairs, you tiptoe down a wide, door-lined corridor on the second floor, stopping occasionally to peep into a darkened room. Tall chairs, elaborately carved tables, and strange paintings of evil-looking men fill the rooms, but the dust is thick over it all. Turning continually to look behind you, you feel the tension rising inside. The hallway makes several turns, and you quickly lose your sense of direction.

The silence is getting on your nerves, and you realize you haven't seen a soul except the halfling.

"Maybe Rorlis has this wing closed for some reason," you say anxiously, as you peer into yet another deserted room.

Finally, the hallway ends at a wide stone staircase that spirals up many floors and also goes down into blackness.

"Let's go up," Tailspin suggests. "I've never been friendly with things that live in black pits."

"If we go up, we might cut off our escape," you say. "And what if Estragon's room is down in the dungeon?"

1) If you decide to go up, turn to page 100.

2) If you decide to go down, turn to page 122.

"A fire is too risky," you say. "I think you should try your spell, Eddas." You send Tailspin and Graypaw to either end of the hall to stand guard.

Eddas looks doubtful but closes his eyes and concentrates. Placing his palms together in front of his chest, he recites a simple illusion spell to make the bees think that you are also bees.

When he finishes, you ask, "How do we know it works?"

"If we go in and the bees don't sting us, then it works," he answers, shrugging.

Taking a deep breath, you edge cautiously into the room. Standing just inside the door, you watch the closest bees, looking for signs that they notice you. Behind you, Eddas whispers, "It seems to be working so far."

You creep toward the door in the opposite wall, zigzagging slightly to imitate a bee's erratic path.

Inevitably, a bee brushes against your leg, and you jump. Tensing for an attack, you relax as it moves away. But another one brushes against Eddas, and then one touches you with its foreleg.

"Do you think they're trying to talk to us?" you ask, as the thought hits you.

"I hope not. The spell doesn't cover bee language," Eddas replies.

You are almost within reach of the door, when several bees surround you, buzzing loudly. "Eddas, are you sure the illusion is working?"

"Maybe they're just offering us honey," he replies, his voice quivering.

The bees block your escape, and suddenly they all start touching you with their forelegs.

"I get the strong impression that we're supposed to answer back," Eddas whispers.

"Oh, no," you groan. "I'll bet they think we're enemy bees from another hive! I never thought of that!" Desperately, you try to edge past them, but you feel a sudden pain in your leg. One of the bees has stung you!

"Ouch!" Eddas cries, grabbing his arm where he, too, was stung. "They're attacking!"

Crying, "Eddas, we've got to get out of here!" you try to push through the ring of bees. But the effects of the stings are already taking place.

"I feel dizzy," Eddas moans, sinking to the floor. The room starts spinning, and you fall beside him. One of the bees lifts you and drops you into a honeycomb chamber.

In a moment of clear thought, you realize the bees are covering the chamber with wax, so you poke a hole in the soft substance to breathe through. You only hope that when the bees sleep at night, you can break through the wax and escape.

THE END

"I don't want to waste Canos's strength," you say. "And that dragon doesn't look very talkative. I say we attack."

You brandish your staff and rush forward, yelling. Slowly, the dragon stands up—and up, and up, and up, and up—and suddenly you feel like a toy man waving a matchstick about the creature's ankles. As it stands, you notice that, enormous as it is, it's on a chain! You desperately wish that you knew how long it is.

Tailspin swoops down and flaps his wings in the dragon's face. Unfortunately, the dragon is so huge that Tailspin can't get in the way of both eyes at once, so the dragon can still see you coming. Graypaw dashes up to the dragon's front leg and runs around it, snarling.

"Look out, Kyol!" Eddas cries.

Too late! A flick of the dragon's clawed foot sends you flying against the wall. Momentarily dazed, you can only watch as Eddas is also batted into the stones.

"Tailspin, get Canos to help!" you cry as you stagger to your feet to escape the dragon's breath of searing fire.

The animals race back for Canos as the dragon slowly reaches out toward you and Eddas—both of you still too groggy for action. Your only hope is Canos, but knowing his condition . . . .

THE END

"Going in through the window should get us right into the thick of things," you say.

You give Tailspin one end of a long rope to carry into the room and loop around a heavy object. He brings you back the end, and you climb the double strand of rope up to the window sill—your arms aching and your stomach grumbling with hunger.

You peer through the window. No one is in the small room, which is full of books and papers. Pulling yourself over the edge, you quickly tie the rope to a heavy table. Leaning out the window, you tell Eddas to tie the rope around Graypaw's middle. Gritting your teeth, you haul the dog up, while he scrambles to keep from banging against the stones.

"Stop cackling, you feathered—OOF!" Graypaw's angry voice floats up to you as he hits the wall—hard!

"Who voted for this fiendish torture?" he groans as you pull him in.

You quickly untie him and drop the rope down to Eddas. Your friend scrambles up and soon hops over the sill.

Eddas asks, "Do you think we can pull my father up? He can't climb with that wounded shoulder."

"Sure," you answer, hoping your arms don't give out at the wrong time.

Canos ties the rope around his waist and, with the two of you pulling, puts his feet on the wall and walks up to the window. Once over the sill, he stands there, exhausted.

"Look around quickly," you say, "before someone shows up."

Graypaw, still in a mood from his humiliating trip up to the window, noses a set of long, ivory bars. "I wonder what these are," he says.

Canos says, "They look like spell-casting rods." Peering around, he comments, "This must be the magician's workroom—it's full of magic books and scrolls."

"I hope he doesn't want to work in here very soon," Eddas says.

"I need to rest. I'll look around here, and get my second wind before I go any farther," Canos says quietly. He is clutching his shoulder, and he looks pale. "You two should explore some of the other rooms and report back to me."

"Right," you say. "We'll also watch the hall, in case someone comes."

You and Eddas take the animals and walk down the hallway. "Do you think it's safe to open every door?" Eddas asks.

"Do you think it's safe to open ANY door?" Tailspin inquires, flying back and forth over your heads.

"Good question," you say, looking around. There are about twelve doors, most of them closed, in the long hall, besides the one you came out of. One end of the hall stops at a window, and at the other end, it turns the corner.

Which way to start? There are so many doors, and this is just one hallway! Confusion turns to frustration, and you feel defeated before you begin.

"This is crazy," you tell your friend. "How can we possibly look in all these rooms and identify the one that moves around?"

"Just relax and use your intuition," Eddas advises. "That's what we practiced so many hours at home."

A soft buzzing noise attracts Eddas's attention. Not sure what it is, he follows it until he gets to a closed door. Beckoning to you, he opens the door slowly.

The buzzing becomes louder. You are staring at a giant hive!

You stare at the giant bees crawling around the honeycomb. The bees are at least as big as you are, and a few are bigger. They are busy filling honeycomb chambers with wax or honey—you're not sure which.

"I'd hate to see the queen bee," Tailspin mutters. "What do you think, Graypaw?" He looks around the room. "Hey! Where's he gone to?"

You hear a faint whine and finally see the dog—under a bench in the hall.

"Ho! You coward!" Tailspin crows. "Now I understand the meaning of 'turn tail and run.' Hah!"

Graypaw snarls back. "That's easy for you to say, you flying feather duster! If you remember, I was seriously injured by bees last summer!"

"Quiet, you two, and let me think," you order. You stare at the hive, wondering if it's a barrier to protect something important.

Suddenly you realize that a door on the far side of the room is open and through it you can see an elf. Estragon! He seems not to pay any attention to the bees, and you wonder if he's under a spell.

"We've got to get through there somehow," you say.

"I've heard that bees are affected by smoke," Eddas says. "Would that help?"

"You could cast a spell making the bees think that we're also bees. Then we could walk right through the room," you say.

"I don't know," Eddas says doubtfully. "Are bees smart or stupid?"

"I don't know," you admit, "but if we start a fire to get smoke, it might bring the guards."

"I don't think there are any guards," Tailspin states firmly.

"Don't be ridiculous, Tailspin!" you say. "Of course there are guards. We've just been lucky so far, that's all."

"Well, we've got to get through to Estragon, no matter how we do it," Eddas says. "What do you want to do, Kyol?"

You hesitate, watching the swarm. How can anyone get past bees like those?

1) If you want to start a fire and smoke them out, turn to page 75.

2) If you decide to have Eddas cast a spell to make the bees think that you are also bees, turn to page 90.

"I don't think I can use the jewel on all of them," you say. "Wait here."

As quietly as you can, you creep along the edge of the room, trying to stay within the shadows. Your heart is in your mouth as you try not to kick any of the trash strewn on the floor. The shadows are thin in one spot, and you hurry past, hoping you won't be seen.

Suddenly you are lifted into the air and carried into the light. A long, hairy arm holds you tightly around the stomach, holding you firm against your struggles. The trolls cheer triumphantly when they see you. Now, you realize, it's much too late to use your magic spells.

The huge troll who grabbed you cries hoarsely, "Save the girl for dessert! Here's the main course!"

THE END

"No, you're probably right, Tailspin. If there is anything in the cellar, it's probably not friendly."

Moving quietly, you climb the stairs up, up, seemingly forever. You are sweating from the exertion of climbing, so tired that you're ready to collapse, when Tailspin says casually, "I assume you've noticed the goblin at the top of the stairs."

"Goblin?" you gasp, gripping your staff more tightly. "Why didn't you tell me sooner?"

"I just got a whiff of him," the hawk answers. "Revolting smell."

Easing up the last few steps, you peek around the corner. There's a goblin leaning against a door, not five feet away from you. The sword at his side seems to identify him as a guard. He's almost as tall as you, and considerably wider. His face is hideously lumpy, and his eyes bulge out. Your pulse quickens, and you can feel your knees shaking as you stare at him. Apparently, he's not expecting anyone to challenge him.

With a cry, you leap forward onto the landing, brandishing your staff. Startled, the goblin swats at you with his hand, knocking you to the floor. The goblin heads for the stairs, but you grab his ankle, and he falls over you, tumbling headlong down the stairs. His cries fade slowly as he falls.

Trying the door, you find that it's locked. "Now what?" you ask.

Tailspin perches on the door frame, then says, "I seem to be sitting on something." He uses his beak to take a key from the top of the door and drops it in your hand.

"Good going!" you tell him. Eagerly, you unlock the door and peer into a large, comfortable room. An elf is sitting in an easy chair, reading. He looks up and shuts his book as you come in.

"My lord Estragon?" you ask, and he nods confirmation. Hurriedly you say, "We don't have much time if we're going to get out of here without them knowing."

"Where's your army, child?" he asks, amazed. "Don't tell me you came here all alone to rescue me!"

"I had no choice, sir," you reply, explaining what happened to your friends.

"Apparently Canos has raised a hero! But now we must rescue the others."

"Others?" you ask, puzzled.

"Yes, my daughter Michelina and my troops are in the dungeon," he replies. "Rorlis knows he is torturing me by letting me live comfortably while my child is suffering."

Together you descend the long, long staircase, with Tailspin on your shoulder. As you reach the bottom, you hear the noises of a celebration coming through an open door. You quickly hide behind some large boxes and peek in. A group of trolls is carousing and singing. More trolls are entering through two doors in the far wall.

"There she is!" Estragon says suddenly. "They've got my daughter!" Then you see a lovely blond elf backed into a corner, being menaced by some trolls.

"Rorlis was bragging to me that he was going to make her his slave," Estragon says bitterly. "I don't think he would allow the trolls to have her. They must have taken her from the dungeon themselves."

"That gives me an idea," you say, excitedly. Trying to make your voice low and gruff, you call out, "Watch it! The Master's coming, and he's angry! Everyone hide!"

There is instant chaos as the trolls scramble for the doors, deserting the girl.

In moments, the place is cleared, and Estragon springs out from behind the boxes, crying, "Michelina!"

As the startled girl rushes into her father's arms, you jump out and run to check the two doors.

"It's all clear now," you say when you return, "but they'll be back as soon as they realize it was a false alarm."

Michelina leads the way to the dungeons as Estragon introduces you and explains your adventures to her.

"Don't you think we have need of him in our village?" he asks her as he finishes.

She looks at you shyly and nods. "I think there would be great demand for his services among the elves."

You grin, embarrassed but pleased. Now, if you can only rescue your friends, you think, everything will be wonderful.

Arriving at the dungeon, Estragon frees his elves from their cells while you explore. The dungeon hall is long and dimly lit, with deep shadows that could hide anything. Shuddering, you walk along, looking for another way out. You catch sight of a narrow wooden staircase, leading up.

"This way!" you call to the elves, who cautiously follow you up the stairs. The steps end at a door, which you open slowly, peering around it. A thick curtain blocks your view. You gently push the curtain aside—and discover you are in the room where you met Sim, the halfling.

"I know the way out from here!" you say, leading them across the room, into the hall, through the tunnel, and out the hidden entrance.

The elves are well on the way to their village before anyone at the castle knows they're gone!

On the road to Estragon's village, the elf plans how you and he will rescue your friends. He also asks you to help him and his troop of elves defeat Rorlis. You quickly agree, certain you can prove to this great elf that his confidence in you, a human, is well placed.

THE END

Afraid that the door might lead to a trap, you dive under the table—just in time.

The door opens, and you hear the sound of small footsteps. The halfling starts to move around the room, cleaning. You hold perfectly still, hoping he won't sweep under the table. After a few minutes, heavier footsteps join the small ones.

"Sim, this place is a shambles!" a deep voice exclaims. "How can I meet with Rorlis in a room so full of dust? Look at this mantelpiece!"

The footsteps move to the fireplace as a small voice murmurs apologies. "Master Salegarth, I've been working in the kitchen for the last six hours. I haven't had a chance to clean in here yet," the halfling says.

"No excuses!" the sorcerer snaps, and you hear him slap the servant. You hold your breath, hoping Tailspin isn't too obvious.

"There's an inch of dust on this fireplace," the voice is interrupted by a loud sneeze and a flutter of wings.

"Move, Tailspin!" you urge silently.

Suddenly there is a thick silence. After a moment of unendurable waiting, you decide to inch out and find out what's going on. But you can't move! Every muscle of your body is frozen, and you're helplessly stuck under the table. Salegarth must have laid a spell on the room, freezing everything in it except himself and Sim. Panic fills your mind, but you can't even tremble.

As you stare straight ahead, a face peers

under the table. "Aha!" the halfling says. "We have large termites, it seems."

A dark, cruel face appears beside the halfling's, and the sorcerer says, "Wonderful! I need a new slave in the kitchen to replace that miserable Bormer. And what would you say to a fine hawk for supper?"

Inside, you know the unbearable pain of fear and desperation—until you remember you still have Bormer's key! Might there be a chance to use it somehow for escape? If not, for Tailspin and you, this is . . .

THE END

"I don't want to get caught in the main hall-way," you say, turning toward the stairs.

On the second floor, you find another corridor, again lined with doors. You open the first door and find a small bedroom.

Canos, worn out, says, "I really must rest. I can put a spell on the door so no one will come in except you, but I do need to sleep."

You and Eddas agree to scout around, then report back. Canos warns you not to try to do anything alone, except look.

You proceed cautiously down the hall. Eddas listens at each door while you keep watch.

"I don't think we'll ever find anything this way," you complain. "Someone will find us before we ever find Estragon."

"The odds were against us from the beginning," Eddas reminds you. "That didn't stop us from starting out on this quest."

Behind the fifth door, a strange clicking sound catches your friend's attention. He calls you over. "What's making that noise?"

"Well, let's see what's in there."

Slowly you open the door and peer inside. The room is filled with skeletons! Bones lie in heaps on the floor, on tables, on chairs. Leaving the two animals outside, you walk slowly into the room, gazing around. Mixed with the tapestried walls and elegantly carved furniture, the skeletons look grotesquely out of place.

"It seems as if they just fell where they stood," Eddas says, touching one of them.

Fear runs down your spine, and your mouth

goes dry. "I don't like the feel of this."

"Maybe this is a storeroom for the sorcerer's creatures," Eddas suggests.

"Well, if he calls any to him, make sure you're out of the way." You laugh nervously.

CRASH! The door suddenly swings shut! Eddas runs over to check. "It's locked!"

The clicking sound begins again, and you whirl around. The skeletons are coming to life! One by one, the skulls rise from the floors and chairs, followed jerkily by collarbones and arms. You back toward the door as each skull swivels to look at you.

"They know we're here!" Eddas gasps.

"What's wrong in there?" Graypaw calls through the door.

"Graypaw, get Canos!" you shout as the skeletons rattle awkwardly to their feet.

Now they're shuffling toward you, grinning, in a loose-jointed, almost comic, macabre dance. Brittle, white fingers reach out to touch you . . . Let this be a spell—one that Canos has the strength to undo! you think desperately.

THE END

"This looks like the main hall," you say. "Why not start here? We're all so tired, it'll be nice just to look at beds!"

You creep down the hall, checking the rooms, and find an open door that leads into a large bedroom. A heavy coat of dust covers several beds and the floor. Despite the dust, the beds look soft and inviting. You can almost feel yourself sinking into the deep mattress.

"This might be a good place to rest," Canos says as he enters.

"Right under Rorlis's nose?" Eddas asks.

Tailspin perches on your staff, complaining. "My eyes are closing. Let's rest somewhere."

Suddenly you hear the sound of clinking metal. From where you are in the doorway, you can see a halfling walking down the hall, carrying a tray of food. "Maybe he's taking it to Estragon!" you whisper, but then your legs fold under you and you add, "or to just anyone." The beds coax you into the room, and you find it hard to concentrate.

"What do you think we should do, Kyol?" Eddas asks, pulling you away from your scattered thoughts.

1) If you want to rest in the room, turn to page 143.

2) If you decide to follow the halfling, turn to page 146.

"Quick, Tailspin, out this door! No sense waiting for trouble to find us," you cry, throwing the door open. A narrow wooden stairway goes straight down into darkness. The smell of damp wood and dank air assaults your nose. Plunging down the stairs, you are followed swiftly by Tailspin. The hawk flaps up dust, which gets in your eyes and throat. You stand, briefly blinded, at the bottom. The silence is broken by a whining, moaning sound.

"Tailspin, be quiet. Someone might hear us."

"I wasn't saying anything."

You freeze. "Then what's that noise?" Scarcely breathing, you listen intently. Someone is crying!

You take a tentative step down a dimly lit hall. It is wide and long, fading off into blackness from which comes a damp and putrid breeze. The breeze moans slightly as it wafts down the hall—or is it something farther down the hall that you hear? Your knees shake slightly as you listen to it. From the stairs, the hall extends in both directions, and the sputtering torches throw weird and fantastic shadows on the walls.

"There could be anything in those shadows," you whisper. Nervously, you notice the torch brackets, carved into grotesque faces that all seem to look right at you! Trying not to think about it, you search for the origin of the crying.

Turning left from the stairs, you move forward cautiously. There are doors on either side of the hall, all with small barred windows. "This must be the dungeon, Tailspin," you whisper.

"Amazing deduction, Master Kyol!"

"You're not helping, you know," you tell him with a frown.

Midway down the hall, you look into a cell and see a young girl. She's been crying for a long time, it seems, from the look of her red and tear-streaked face, a face that is definitely elven. She is wearing a torn and muddy pale blue gown. Thick, golden braids hang down to her waist. Sitting on a maroon velvet cloak, she stares at the wall, not seeing you.

Clearing your throat, you introduce yourself, asking, "Would you know anything about an elven prince being held here?"

Jumping unsteadily to her feet, she stumbles to the door and eagerly thrusts her fingers through the barred window. "Yes, his name is Estragon, and he's my father! The evil warlord Rorlis captured us as we traveled the mountain pass. He has me locked down here with the rats until I agree to serve him. Twenty of Estragon's soldiers are being held in another hall of the dungeon."

You look around quickly, "Where are the guards?" you ask.

"There are none; they fear to come down here. Anyway, Rorlis knows I cannot escape."

The hairs on your neck rise as you try not to wonder why the guards are afraid. You examine the door and see there is no lock.

"His evil magician locked the door, and I cannot break the spell," she says.

"Oh, great," you mutter. "Only a sorcerer's spell to break."

"Let me get my cloak," she says, retreating to the back of the cell.

Something tells you to check her story. Listening to your intuition, you pull on the cell door. It opens! Suspiciously, you shut it again before she returns.

"Um—are you sure he locked it?" you ask, staring at her.

"If it isn't locked, my name isn't Michelina," she replies vehemently.

"When was the last time you checked your birth certificate?" Tailspin inquires.

"Quiet, bird!" you order, and he flies from your staff, settling gingerly on a torch bracket.

You study Michelina's face. She seems to be telling the truth. But who can say anything for sure, in this strange and evil castle?

1) If you decide to believe her, and open the door again, turn to page 152.

2) If you don't trust her, and decide to leave, turn to page 139.

"Speed is important to us," you say. "I'm taking the road." Charging down toward the orc camp, you hope you can get there before the orcs are alerted. The bushes conceal the charred landscape beyond the road as you gallop toward the oak trees. Without warning, a band of orcs spring onto the road directly in front of your horse, screaming wildly. Your horse bolts, throwing you off and leaving you lying, stunned, in the dust.

Before you can struggle to your feet, Tailspin swoops down and grabs your staff. "Get up, Master Kyol!" he shouts, "Take your staff!" But the orcs pull you up before you can move. Eddas's sword falls out of your pack and into the bushes, unnoticed.

Tailspin sees that you're caught and flies away, still holding your staff. Furiously, you scold yourself for being so foolish. What good are you to your friends now? Frustration boils in you, but you can see no possibility of escape.

Gripping you tightly, the orcs argue about what to do with you.

"Kill him, I say," one orc shouts, "and take his valuables."

"He's dressed like an elf," an orc comments nervously. "The Master said all elves are to be taken alive."

"We'd better take him to the camp," another says.

Their discussion soon confirms that there is indeed an evil magician working against the elves. Could it possibly be Mycrose the Demon,

from the East? As far as you know, there are no evil sorcerers in the land other than Salegarth, at the castle, and Mycrose, who lives among the orcs in the East. But why would he come here? you wonder.

You are given no opportunity to ask as the orcs force you to trot the long road to camp. The entrance to the camp, which is underground as you suspected, is hidden behind a clump of bushes. Even the guards aren't visible until you get all the way to the bushes. You realize you'd have been spotted long before you found them. The scent of horses comes from a smaller cave mouth, and the orcs lead your horse off in that direction.

Leading you down a dark tunnel, they push you into a small prison cell. The damp walls are slimy to the touch, and there's barely enough room for you to pace two steps in any direction. Gingerly, you sit in the middle of the cell.

"Stay there until the Master decides what to do with you," an orc chortles, locking the door. Alone in the silence, exhausted and afraid, you try to think of some way out. Unfortunately, the rigors of the trip have worn you out, and you quickly fall into a restless sleep.

Please turn to page 47.

"I still think you're going to be in big trouble!" Your hawk's voice is harsh with worry.

"Listen, Tailspin, if I had stayed home, I'd be of no use to anyone. This way, at least I can still help Canos and Eddas."

The black hawk on your shoulder flaps his wings angrily, ruffling your hair. "It's all very well for you, Master Kyol, but Canos is liable to turn me into a mouse. I'll be eaten by my own people!"

You chuckle softly and slowly rein in your horse. Grasping your staff securely, you feel for the amulet safely hidden under your shirt in a green silk bag hanging from a gold cord around your neck. The staff and amulet are the only weapons you carry, but you feel confident that they're enough. Gazing around, you stretch your tired arms.

"We should be nearing the Pass of Laedris," you tell Tailspin. "The road gets very rocky after that, according to elven maps. I wonder if Canos and Eddas have gotten that far."

After two days of following the caravan, you're not even sure how far ahead they are. The long grasses of the valley have given way to the brown scrub brush of the low hills. This is orc territory, and you're on the alert for roving bands of marauders. As a lone rider, you would make a good target. A chill wind sweeps down from the mountains ahead of you, and you shiver. The sun ducks in and out of the clouds as you search for signs of the elves' passage.

"Darn those elven eyes! If they couldn't see

so far, I could keep a closer tail on Eddas."

"Do you want me to fly ahead?"

"No, it'd be just our luck that they'd recognize you."

"That insolent Graypaw certainly would. He's had it in for me for a long time."

"You're lucky to have—"

Suddenly the clash of steel on steel rings thinly through the still morning air. Your horse shies, and you struggle to hold it down. Faint cries and shouts echo up from beyond the next hill, but you see nothing disturbing the peaceful scenery.

"Tailspin! There's a fight! I'd better go to help!"

"What if it's not Canos, but just some orcs fighting the natives?"

1) If you decide it's not your friends and to keep out of the fight, turn to page 16.

2) If you decide it is the elves, and you ride forward to help, turn to page 31.

"This potion is just what I need to fight Rorlis," you decide. You uncap the bottle and drink deeply.

Nothing happens for a minute, and you're disappointed. But you attempt to pick up the small table and discover it only takes one hand. "I must be stronger," you cry. But, strangely enough, the table is shrinking. Or is it? You glance around the room and discover that you're growing!

"Oh, no!" you cry. "*Great* meant *big*, not *strong*!" Your voice booms out, rattling the windows.

Within minutes you are too big to get out the door. You have to duck to avoid the ceiling, and your feet are knocking over the tables. Frightened, you tuck yourself into a ball, with your face near the door.

You watch as the wolfhound returns. It sniffs the open door, then catches sight of you. Yelping, it tucks its tail between its legs and streaks off.

In a couple of minutes, Tailspin flies up the stairs, calling your name. You call back, but your gigantic voice sounds like an explosion. Tailspin alights and sees your enormous eye peering out the door.

"Awk!" he cries. "A monster's eaten Kyol! My poor master!" Squawking, he flies away.

Squeezed painfully into the cramped room, you hope the potion wears off before Rorlis comes to get it for himself. Perhaps you drank too much. . . .

THE END

"I'd feel safer on the ground floor," you say. "Let's go down."

After a long, winding descent, you begin to hear voices. A faint light glows from the bottom of the stairwell.

"I don't like this," Tailspin mutters, sitting on your shoulder.

"Shh!" you say. "We've come this far, so let's see what's here."

At the bottom, you find you are stopped by a pile of boxes that blocks your view. Peering over, you see a large group of trolls, drinking and singing terrible songs. The edges of the room are shadowy in places, but the center is lit with blazing torches.

There must be fifty trolls in the smoky, trash-filled room, and most of them are armed. You shudder as you hear them sing, "Rip off his arm and bite off his head, tear him apart and make sure he's dead!" You look around for a way out, other than back up the stairs. Then you see her!

On the far side of the room, a terrified young elven girl is backed into a corner. Her long blond braids swing free to her waist, and her pale blue gown is torn and muddy. She's standing with her back to the wall, trapped by a grinning monster of a troll. You suspect that the trolls are planning to eat her!

"What can we do?" you whisper.

"Why don't you use the Jewel of Kaibak?" Tailspin suggests.

"I was saving it for an emergency," you say, quickly terrified at the thought of using it.

"Don't you think this qualifies?" the bird asks.

"Maybe if I sneak around the edge of the room, they won't notice me."

"They might smell you," Tailspin says.

You pause, your heart beating wildly. Tailspin has a good point, but you also know that the jewel can be terribly dangerous to use. Still, you've braved so many other dangers that maybe you do have the courage now. Your tired brain refuses to think clearly, and you wish desperately that Canos were here to advise you. But you know that you're alone and have to make your own decision.

1) If you decide to use the Jewel of Kaibak to try to make the trolls fight among themselves, turn to page 135.

2) If you would rather to sneak around the edge of the room, turn to page 99.

"I'd better not take any chances," you decide, and you pocket the bottle.

Tailspin flies up a moment later. "That was close!" he exclaims. "I had to dig my claws into stone and pretend to be a torch bracket. Before that, I almost lost my tail feathers to that silly dog!"

"Not again!" you laugh.

"It's not funny," he retorts. "Listen, as I was flying down the hall, I heard loud voices from the top of a staircase. It could be trouble."

"Or it could be Estragon," you say. "Lead the way."

Tailspin guides you down a long hall ending at a staircase. Creeping up the steps, you come to the open door of a large tower room filled with fine furniture. You peer cautiously in and see a heavyset man with a black beard, arguing with a tall elf.

You step back into the hall and whisper to Tailspin, "I think it's Estragon and Rorlis!" Then, taking a chance, you turn and creep into the room. You study Rorlis carefully as you edge toward a table near an open window. The warlord is wearing dark green pants and a matching jacket, the jacket open to accommodate his massive chest. His gleaming black boots have obviously been polished diligently. A pearl-handled sword in a jewel-encrusted scabbard hangs from his wide belt.

He must have spent years collecting—or robbing—to gather such finery. With his gray-flecked hair, he looks older than Estragon, but you know that the elf has lived for many generations.

"If you let me have the weapon, Estragon, I will give your daughter a room as comfortable as yours," the warlord bargains, "instead of that cold, rat-ridden dungeon where she has to sleep on the stones."

"No," replies Estragon. "It's too powerful to be in your hands, Rorlis. You can't sway me by torturing my daughter."

"Now is the time," you think. "How do I distract him?" You know if you try to fight, Rorlis will probably kill you. Desperately, you glance around the room, then out the window, looking for inspiration. Then you grin. You've got an idea!

"Excuse me," you break in, and the warlord turns, angry at being interrupted.

You hold the bottle out the window, as if you're going to drop it. "How much is this magic potion worth?"

Rorlis pales and takes a step toward you, but you quickly warn him. "I'll drop it if you come any closer."

As Rorlis hesitates, Estragon spins him around and sends him flying with a strong punch. Not giving the warlord a chance to unsheathe his sword, the elf jumps him. They roll around the floor in a mighty struggle. You can only stand and watch. In your excitement, you almost knock over a tall pitcher on the table, but you catch it in time.

For a moment, Estragon rocks back, momentarily stunned, and you watch in horror as Rorlis jumps up, his hand on the sword in his belt. You quickly grab the pitcher, step behind the warlord, and hit him as hard as you can. He falls to the floor, groaning.

"Good work, young man," Estragon says. "Did you come here alone to rescue me? What about my daughter and my troops in the dungeon?"

"There are others in the dungeon? Rorlis only mentioned your daughter," you say, surprised.

You tell him what happened to Canos and Eddas, explaining that you didn't know about the other elves. Estragon listens as he ties the warlord securely and drags him to his feet. Forcing Rorlis to show you the way, you proceed quickly down the stairs toward the dungeon, all the while telling your tale.

At the opening to a dark tunnel, Rorlis stops. "The dungeon is that way," he says, "but you'll just have needless trouble if your troops see me too soon. Tie me up and I'll wait for you here."

"Shall I fly ahead and check it out, Master Kyol?" Tailspin asks.

"No, wait a moment," you say. Your intuition tells you Rorlis is being less than honest. Suspiciously, you take out your amulet, the dark green, owl-shaped gemstone that glows with a warm inner light. Asking Estragon to wait, you gaze into the gem and let your mind follow the light as you concentrate on the truth.

Suddenly, in your mind's eye, you see a grue-

some blob of black jelly, oozing along a dark hall. The bones of its victim are scattered on the floor.

"He's lying," you say. "There's a black blob down that hall, waiting to destroy us."

Rorlis pales as you speak, and Estragon turns to him angrily. "I warn you, Rorlis, do not lie to me a second time."

"Now, Rorlis," Estragon says, "direct us to where you've hidden our weapons, and remember the consequences of lying!"

Rorlis gives you a glance, and you try to look fierce. Apparently convinced of your power, the warlord leads you quickly to the weapons storeroom.

Estragon's elves, now fully armed, spread out to take control of the castle. Then you ask Estragon's help in rescuing your friends.

"I'll go with you myself," he says, smiling. "I'll leave Michelina in charge of the castle and send Rorlis, with some of my men, back to my village for trial."

And so, with the legendary leader at your side, you set off to rescue Eddas and Canos.

THE END

"She's riding a unicorn, so she can't be evil. Unicorns never allow anyone evil to ride them, as far as I know," you tell Eddas. "I think we should tell her."

You explain your journey and your purpose, and she looks thoughtful. "You might be able to succeed," she says slowly.

"Do you own this castle?" you ask.

She smiles sadly. "I am Alesa. Once my king and I ruled it together. That was before the evil warlord Rorlis killed my king and imprisoned me here."

"Alesa!" Canos cries. "We wondered what happened to you."

"Rorlis has been trying to make me agree to serve him, but I've refused all these years—and so remained a captive in his garden. It's the thornbushes: Should I approach that wall, the thorns, under Salegarth's evil spell, become a thousand swords, aimed and ready to run me through."

Suddenly she smiles. "But I have a secret that Rorlis doesn't know about."

She reaches behind her and presents you with a shield, the arm strap facing you. The shield is round, with red leather bindings and polished silver studs. "This is a magic shield. It will instantly paralyze anyone who looks into it and then turn them to stone," she says. "I would have used it sooner, but I have no allies here."

You take the shield and then promise to return for her.

"Rorlis has bragged that Estragon's room

cannot be easily found," she says. "The sorcerer Salegarth moves the room around the castle periodically, so it could be almost anywhere. You'll have to use magic to locate it, I'm afraid." She points out the spell-locked gate from the garden to the castle. Canos whispers a spell, waving his arms, and the white gate swings open.

Giving Alesa hope that she will soon be free, you and your friends enter a hallway. Very quickly it divides.

"I can use my powers to decide which way to go," Canos says, "but I'll be completely spent after that. You'll have to rescue him yourselves." He furrows his brow and concentrates deeply. Sweat forms on his face as he casts outward for Estragon's presence. Finally he opens his eyes. "This way," he says, leading you forward.

Your party encounters no guards during your search, and you're getting nervous. "Why are there no guards?" you ask.

"One Salegarth is worth a hundred guards," Graypaw mumbles, "if he's up to par."

After climbing a long flight of stairs, you round a corner, right into a pair of goblins who are guarding a door.

"You didn't warn us, Canos," you say, quickly raising your staff.

"I was concentrating on Estragon," he says, wearily slumping onto the top step.

You and Eddas parry furiously with the guards, who are much huskier than you. Graypaw dives through the legs of the taller goblin, and he lands on his back with a scream. Eddas leans forward to hit him and receives a sword thrust in his shoulder.

"Don't look, Eddas!" you cry, freeing yourself from the battle and holding up the shield. The goblins glance up at it and freeze, turning to stone instantly.

"Are you all right, Eddas?" you ask, quickly putting the shield away.

"Yes, fine. Just don't ask me to do a handstand."

You break open the door and rush in. The room is large and with thick carpets and elegant furniture. Estragon rises from a chair, and you explain who you are.

"This doesn't look like a prison cell," Tailspin comments suspiciously.

"Rorlis thinks he can break me faster by letting me live in luxury while my daughter and troops are suffering in the dungeon," Estragen says bitterly.

"We'll rescue them as soon as we can," you assure him. "But now we must move—someone may have heard us fighting."

Quickly you return to the garden. "This shield is wonderful," you say, "but I can't use it against an entire army. Does anyone have any ideas?"

"Kyol!" Eddas cries. "Use the Jewel of Kaibak! I'd do it myself, but I'm wounded." Canos nods his approval, too weary to speak.

"I don't know," you say, hesitating. You can

feel the familiar fear washing over you as you think of how you could ruin your brain. But you remember the problems you've overcome so far, and you relax a bit. Nervously you place the gold bracelet on your arm.

Concentrating all your energies on the sparkling red jewel, you strain to include everyone in the castle, except those in the garden, in the spell. Focusing on the blood-red stone, you feel yourself breaking into the center of the jewel's power and aiming it outward.

Suddenly a great shout goes up from the castle, and the sounds of battle are heard everywhere. You smile in weary triumph at your friends. Once again, you have used the dangerous Jewel of Kaibak and succeeded.

"Well done, young Kyol," Canos murmurs.

After several hours, the sounds of battle cease, and you venture out to look. The troops of Rorlis have defeated each other, and the castle is free!

"Now we must free my daughter and troops from the dungeon," Estragon says.

Your party, with Queen Alesa leading, locates the dungeon and releases the elves. A joyful Michelina rushes into Estragon's arms. "Father, are you all right?" she asks.

"Yes, fine, thanks to our brave friends."

"We must make sure Rorlis hasn't escaped," Canos says, and the other elves agree. Splitting up, you and Tailspin search the castle, which is now silent and empty.

Suddenly the silence is broken by the sound

of footsteps in a room up ahead of you. "Is it one of the elves?" you wonder aloud.

"Or someone else?" Tailspin responds.

Gripping your staff, you creep down the hall toward the door. Gathering your courage, you fling it open.

A heavyset, black-bearded man stands holding a dusty old book. He is dressed in dark green, with a sword at his belt. You know it must be Rorlis. Somehow, he has escaped the spell.

Tailspin leaves your shoulder as you raise your staff. Rorlis reaches for his sword, but you rush forward and land a good, strong blow. He staggers, groaning, but recovers and throws at you the book he was holding. You duck, and in that moment he draws his sword.

"So, little one," he crows. "We'll see who will leave this room alive."

You block his blows, then give him a sharp whack on the side of his knee, and he staggers. Grabbing the advantage, you swing the staff and knock him unconscious.

"You've done it!" Tailspin cries. "You have defeated Rorlis alone!" The others run up.

"Congratulations, Kyol!" Eddas cries. "You're a real hero now!"

"My thanks to you, Kyol," Queen Alesa says. "You will always be welcome here in Friendship Castle."

You are tired but proud and happy that you have learned well how to serve your friends.

THE END

"You're right. I can't battle them all if they sniff me out. And I've got to try the Jewel of Kaibak sometime—if I don't want to be a coward for life."

You place the gold band holding the jewel on your arm. Keenly aware that if you don't do it right, your brain will be ruined, you breathe deeply several times, calming your nerves and mind. Concentrating all your energy on the jewel, you try to guide your mind into the correct path for control.

The world goes fuzzy around you as you look deeper into the bloodred gem. Soon it feels as if you are swimming in icy water, moving closer and closer to the center of power. Vague shapes swirl around you, but you shut out the distractions and focus on the force that is pulling you toward it. Abruptly, you are inside the center of power, away from the swirling shapes. The spell takes form and moves out toward the room.

Vague sounds penetrate your concentration as you finish, and you realize that you've succeeded: the trolls are fighting! Risking a look, you see them scuffling, clawing each other viciously.

"It works!" Tailspin cries above the noise. The trolls have forgotten the girl, and she is easing around them, heading for you.

"We've got to get out of here fast," you whisper as she reaches you.

"But we must rescue my father first," she says.

"Estragon is your father?" you ask. She nods.

"My name is Michelina. They've hidden my father in a room that can move from place to place, even from floor to floor, and they locked me in a dungeon. The trolls dragged me from there and said they were going to eat me. I don't think Rorlis knows they did it."

"Where should we look for your father?" you ask.

"We can start at the tower," she replies. "That's where the room was when I last saw him."

Together you climb the hundreds of steps to the tower, pausing often to catch your breath. "I'm afraid," you gasp, clutching your side, "that when we get there, I'll be too tired to rescue him." Michelina nods, too winded to speak.

Tailspin, sitting on your shoulder, says, "I can't see why you're so fatigued after only a few steps."

"Quiet, bird," you say, "or you'll get no more free rides."

At the top of the stairs, two goblins are guarding the door. "Now I'm sure he's in there," Michelina says.

You concentrate on the jewel again, just enough to get the two guards bickering. They stamp off, one of them crying, "I'll show you who's the stronger!"

Breaking open the door, you enter Estragon's room, and Michelina rushes into his arms. You explain your adventures quickly to the startled elf. "I'm very grateful to you for rescuing my daughter," he says.

"We still have to get out of here," you reply.

"My men are locked up in the dungeon. If we can free them, we might be able to overcome Rorlis," Estragon tells you eagerly.

"Then let's not waste any time," you say, leading the way back down the steps. Tailspin flies ahead of you. Your legs are about to give out, but you are afraid of the consequences of resting.

In the basement room, most of the trolls are dead or unconscious. Michelina leads you past them to the dungeon holding the elven troops.

Estragon quickly frees them and then says, "Now we must capture Rorlis!"

"But how can we fight an entire castle with only twenty elves?" you ask.

"You've got a point, Master Kyol," Tailspin says, perched on your staff.

"Why don't you use that jewel again?" Michelina asks.

You take out the Jewel of Kaibak and stare at it. A few trolls and goblins are one thing, but an entire castle . . . ! You felt very lucky to escape unscathed the first two times. Weak and tired as you are, you don't know if you can do it again.

"If you have already used the Jewel of Kaibak, you are a more powerful magic-user than I thought," Estragon says in admiration.

Encouraged by his obvious respect for your talent, you make up your mind and put the jewel on your arm. Willing yourself to stay calm, you concentrate with the last bit of your energy. Just when you think you can't push any farther, you break into the center of power and direct it toward the castle.

Shouts come from everywhere as the castle comes alive with the sounds of battle. Weary, you wait with the elves until the fighting dies down. Then, moving swiftly, the elves round up what's left of Rorlis's troops. Rorlis himself is found trying to escape through the main gate. He's captured and bound, to be brought to the elves' village for trial.

As he prepares to leave, Estragon takes you aside. "Would you consent to stay and command the guard here just until I return with reinforcments?" he asks you.

Flattered, you tell him you'd be proud to do it, but you have to rescue Eddas and Canos. Estragon promises to free them himself and send them to join you at the castle.

As the elven leader leaves, he hints that you will be entitled to a large reward. But you know that the best reward will be seeing your friends again and knowing that you didn't disappoint them.

THE END

It might be a trick, you think, wondering if she could be a sorceress in disguise. Surely if Estragon's daughter had been captured, Prince Novoye would have mentioned it when he appointed Canos to rescue Estragon.

"I—I don't think I can break the spell," you tell her, avoiding her eyes.

"Oh." Michelina is crestfallen. "If you can't do that, there's no sense in sending you through the magic portal to my father."

Suspecting another trap, you say nothing and walk away, feeling bad about leaving her.

Walking swiftly down the hall, you come to a divided passage. The right branch is high enough for a man to walk upright, but it's littered with rocks and other obstacles. You don't examine them too closely, fearing that they may be the gruesome remains of something. The left passage is very narrow and appears to get smaller as it proceeds.

You enter the right-hand corridor and find it badly lit. Deep shadows obscure the path. Soft grunts and moans echo softly, but you can't pinpoint the source. As usual, there are many doors opening off the corridor, but you stop looking in after running into several cobwebbed skeletons. You follow the hall for almost a half-hour, randomly turning corners when it branches into more passages.

You choose a left branch, then a right, then another branch. After a time, you realize you're not sure of how to get back. Weary and confused, you slump to the floor, next to a pile of rags. Your

legs and back ache, and you're so hungry you could eat almost anything, cooked or raw! Why hadn't you thought to bring food with you? You desperately want to take a nap, but you don't know what might lurk in this passage. Are the eerie noises getting louder, or is it your imagination?

As you realize how lost you are, you think, "I certainly hope Tailspin knows where HE is."

Glancing at the rag pile, you realize that it's actually a crumpled skeleton. You shudder as you wonder if this was another unfortunate who got lost—perhaps eaten by the tunnel's inhabitants! You're almost too tired to be afraid, but you know that, sooner or later, something is going to come along that passage. To fight it, you'll need strength, and right now you can't even stand up . . . .

THE END

If the potion is that well guarded, it must be worth having," you say thoughtfully. "See if you can distract the dog." And Tailspin flies warily off.

A moment later, the hawk comes whizzing back around the corner, pursued by a huge, dark wolfhound. As the two race past, you move swiftly around the corner to a large door with a handle but no lock.

Rorlis has a lot of confidence in that dog, you think, pulling on the smooth iron latch. The door creaks open, and you tiptoe in, watching for booby-traps.

The room is tiny, about five feet by seven feet, with one small window that gives little light. The stone walls are hung with large tapestries, and several small tables are cluttered with knickknacks.

Trembling in your haste, you sort through the jumble of objects, not sure what you're looking for. Canos kept all his potions in clear vials, but there's no guarantee that the warlord does the same.

A tiny green bottle catches your eye, and you pick it up. The label reads: "Potion of Power. Drink me and be great."

1) If you want to drink the potion to become "great" and fight the warlord, turn to page 120.

2) If you want to take it with you to use later, turn to page 124.

"I guess we all need a rest, and we probably won't be disturbed here," you say, sinking gratefully onto a bed. The others choose their beds, and soon you can hear gentle snoring.

Before you drift off, you decide to close the door so you'll have some warning if someone comes in. Struggling to get out of the soft covers, you realize, terror-stricken, that a magic spell has you in its grip, holding you on the bed, incredibly sleepy. Frantically, you watch as the door closes softly by itself.

"A mad and brilliant trap," you think, as your eyes get too heavy to hold open, and you drift away into an endless sleep.

THE END

"Let's find out what the noise is first," you say, slowly opening the door.

A group of black-robed figures, facing away from you, chants softly. As your gaze moves to the front of the room, you notice a ghostly blue giant sitting cross-legged on a cushion. The black-robed group must be worshipping him.

"It's a djinn!" Eddas whispers. "Djinni are very dangerous except for their masters."

The djinn's eyes meet yours as he notices you for the first time. His hand moves too swiftly to follow, and suddenly you're not holding onto the door anymore. You're flapping small black wings and hovering six feet off the ground. You squeak at the others and discover that you have all been changed into bats!

As you fly down the hall together, you hope that even as a bat Canos has not lost his powers, and that he can think of a way to break this spell.

THE END

"I think we should follow the halfling and rest later," you say. Tiptoeing quietly, you watch as the little servant walks swiftly down the hall. Stopping before a closed door, he taps the wall at about shoulder height, three times. Then he opens the door and enters, leaving the door ajar.

"A booby-trapped door?" you ask, following. When you look warily through the door, all you see is a hallway, ending at another door, where you see the halfling bending over.

"What's he doing?" Graypaw asks.

"He reached under the carpet and pushed a button," Eddas replies. The door swings open, revealing a narrow staircase. The halfling ascends quickly, and the door swings quietly shut behind him. You hurry over to listen at the door as the sound of his footsteps fades.

"Hurry, Kyol," Tailspin says. You find the patch of rug, lift it, and push the button. The door opens silently, and you see the halfling's feet disappearing above you.

Carefully, you lead the way up the steps, hoping they don't creak. You reach the top in time to see the halfling pulling the tassel of a hanging rope. Suddenly the far wall slides open, revealing a door. The halfling fishes in his pocket for a key and unlocks the door. As it opens and he walks in, you catch sight of Estragon!

"Good work!" Eddas whispers.

You charge into the room as the halfling is placing the tray on a table. The startled servant tries to escape into the hall, but you grab him by the collar.

Looking around, you see that the room is large, and thick rugs cover the floor. Elegant furniture fills the room, and an open window lets in bright sunlight.

"Canos!" Estragon cries, rushing forward.

The halfling struggles in your arms. "You're not going anywhere," you say, "except to lead us out of this castle."

"I will if you spare my life," the halfling squeaks.

"Then let's go, halfling."

"First we must rescue my daughter and my men from the dungeon," Estragon says. "Rorlis put them there while leaving me in comfort. He knows it hurts me to have the others suffer."

The halfling leads you back around the booby traps and down into the dungeon, "Salegarth the sorcerer put a spell on the elves," he says. "They think the cell doors are locked, but they're not."

When you arrive at the dungeon, Estragon frees his elves and then his daughter, who rushes into his arms.

"Michelina, are you all right?" he asks, hugging her. She nods, smiling. Her long blond braids hang to her waist, and her pale blue dress is torn and muddy.

"Hurry! We must get to the weapons storeroom," says the halfling, now eager to help.

You follow him to the first-floor storeroom. When the elves have chosen weapons, Estragon says, "Spread out and find Rorlis. I want him captured, not dead."

You and Eddas search the second floor. At the end of a hallway, you find a staircase.

"We may never find our way out of here," Graypaw complains as he lopes behind Eddas.

"I have a perfect sense of direction," Tailspin announces. "To return, we simply have to go down."

"Brilliant thinking," Graypaw mutters.

Looking around, you see a long torch-lit hall lined with narrow tables and tall chairs. Closed doors line both sides of the hall.

You are halfway down the hall, when a door bursts open and a heavyset black-bearded man rushes straight into you!

"Wha—what are you doing here?" he demands, his hand on the sword at his belt.

"It must be Rorlis!" Tailspin cries excitedly. You raise your staff and hold it across your chest as protection.

Eddas brandishes his sword and says, "Surrender, Rorlis, or we'll attack."

"Hah!" the warlord laughs heartily. "Do you think I'm afraid of you children?" He starts to draw his sword, but you swing quickly and catch him in the shoulder. Staggering, he growls, "Now I'm angry!" Drawing his sword, he swings as you duck. Eddas meets the warlord's sword with his own, and the clash of steel rings through the hall.

Graypaw streaks past Eddas and charges into Rorlis, biting him viciously on the leg.

"You miserable cur!" the warlord cries. "I'll get you—OW!" he cries as Tailspin's sharp claws tear into his arm, forcing him to drop his weapon. Before Rorlis can reach for his sword, Eddas's blade is at his throat.

"Surrender, Rorlis!" you cry. "You've been defeated by two children, no less."

Angrily, the warlord surrenders, and you quickly tie him up with his own belt and lead him back downstairs.

You turn to Eddas and say, "Nice going, friend."

"We worked as a team," he replies, smiling.

"I . . . uh . . . appreciate your saving my life," Graypaw tells Tailspin awkwardly.

Embarrassed, the hawk replies gruffly, "With you gone, I'd have no one to torment."

"Then you admit it!" the dog yelps. "Did you hear that, Master Eddas? He admits that his vile comments are meant to torment me!"

You and Eddas laugh heartily. "I didn't think their sudden friendliness would last long," you say.

Eddas grins. "Well, if we have anything to do with it, they'll be having adventures together for a long while!"

Both animals groan, and you laugh, knowing that this is just the first of many exciting adventures of four good friends.

THE END

"If she lives here, we can't trust her," you whisper to Eddas.

Raising your staff to look menacing, you demand safe passage through the garden. But the woman who calls herself Alesa brings forth a mirrored shield. You glance into its depths, and the words freeze in your throat. You try to tear your gaze away, but your eyes are locked into the mirror.

"It would have been better if you had trusted me," she says, and she rides away on her unicorn.

As you stand paralyzed, you now understand why there are so many statues in her garden.

THE END

She definitely looks like an elf, and there's a chance she can lead you to Estragon, so you decide to believe her. Swinging the door wide, you say, "The magician put a spell on you, not on the door."

Michelina's eyes widen in surprise, and she blushes. "It . . . it really was locked," she stammers.

"I believe you," you say smiling. "Now, let's find your father."

Michelina leads you down the dim hallway, whispering, "I was brought here through a magic portal in this wall." Suddenly remembering, she asks, "Should we look for my father's troops first?"

"How many can go through the portal at one time?" you ask.

"Rorlis sent through only two at a time," she replies.

"Then we should rescue your father first. With a whole troop of elves, we'd be seen or heard long before we could get clear away," you decide.

With Tailspin guarding the far passage, she concentrates on locating the hidden door. The effort makes her slightly unsteady, and she says weakly, "This would be easier if I weren't so hungry and cold." Finally, she moves to a blank spot of wall between two doors. "Here it is," she says, feeling for the latch.

"The secret passage leads directly to the room where Estragon is being held, by a jump through a magic portal," she explains. "The warlord told me that the sorcerer Salegarth has placed a spell on the room, causing it to move around. The portal is the one fast way for Rorlis to locate Estragon's room, wherever it is."

You step warily through the place she indicates on the wall, and for a moment, you have an odd sensation of nonexistence. Then you're back in the real world again, the real world of a large closet. Tailspin pops into the closet a moment later. Before he can complain, you grab his beak and hiss, "Quiet! We don't know what's out there!"

As you push the door open a few inches, you catch sight of the great elf, Estragon himself, sitting at a table. The room is spacious and comfortable looking. Books are stacked on the large table in the center, and a wide bed is pushed against the far wall. You can't see to the right, but the left wall has a large door in it.

"Rorlis is keeping his hostage in good shape," you whisper, "but that doesn't apply to the rest of the elves." Michelina nods grimly. "He knows it hurts my father more to see us suffer than to suffer himself." Changing the subject abruptly, she says, "The guards are outside the main door, I think." Quietly, you sneak in.

"Father!" Michelina cries softly and runs into her startled father's arms.

"Wha . . . where did you come from?" he asks, amazed.

You introduce yourself and explain how you arrived here.

"I'm overjoyed that you rescued my daugh-

ter, but I'm grieved to hear about my friend Canos's predicament," he says.

"I was hoping you'd be able to rescue them if I can get you out of here," you say.

"Certainly, if we can get out. I'm afraid that magic passage is sealed from this direction."

You try the closet portal and discover he's right. "If Canos were here, he could unlock it," you say, frustrated. "I guess our only chance is to overpower the guards."

You wait beside the door as Estragon grabs a heavy, metal inkstand from among the stacks of books, then calls the two goblin guards. They walk in, cautiously but not really expecting trouble. Moving swiftly, Canos strikes at one goblin, and you knock out the other. You both leap out into the hall, alert for other enemies, but the path is clear. Then you hurry the elves down the hall, with Tailspin riding on your shoulder.

"We must free my troops," Estragon says.

"They're locked in another wing of the dungeon," Michelina tells him.

"Any idea which way that is?" you ask.

"Down, of course, silly," Michelina replies.

You meet no one as you silently descend the stairs and search for a way into the dungeon. Finally, you recognize the hall as the one where you saw the halfling.

"This way!" you say confidently, opening the door.

The same halfling that you saw earlier is busy wiping the table, and he squeaks in horror as you enter. Grabbing him quickly, you tie him up with his own cleaning cloth and leave him in a corner as you draw the curtain, opening the secret door to the stairway.

When you get to the bottom of the stairs, Michelina points to the right, away from her old cell. "They're somewhere down there," she says.

"I'll let them out," Estragon says. "You wait here."

Nervously, you, Michelina, and Tailspin wait by the stairs for Estragon. Suddenly Michelina sees a dim figure approaching.

"It's Rorlis!" Michelina cries. "He's followed us!"

"Apparently, he can use the portal both ways," you say tensely—and then realize you'll have to stop him! "Get Estragon, you two," you order, moving forward to block Rorlis's path.

"You little pip-squeak, let me by!" the warlord orders, not even bothering to unsheathe his sword. His black hair and dark green clothes make him hard to see in the dimly lit hall. Not for the first time, you wish you had elven eyes.

Holding your staff in front of you for protection, you say, "Stop right there, Rorlis! Without your troops to help, you'll never get past me!"

He laughs and moves closer. "Child! Neither you nor that elf is a match for me. Move aside, before I get angry." As he steps toward you, you slam the staff against the side of his head. Dazed, he fumbles for his sword, but a swift crack to his inner elbow numbs his arm.

"Brat!" He curses, struggling to draw his

sword with his other hand. But you quickly manage to land two strong blows to his chest, and he falls to the floor, gasping.

As Rorlis stumbles to his feet, Estragon and his elves rush up. They tie and gag him, using their own belts and laces.

"That was very brave," Estragon says to you as your party climbs the steps, dragging Rorlis behind. When you enter the room, you add the halfling to your group. Then you lead the way through the four-foot-high tunnel through which you entered the castle when you found your way in originally.

You and the elves set off on foot for Cillisan, with only Tailspin riding your horse, which has the enraged warlord in tow!

"After you free Canos and Eddas," Estragon says, "I would be happy if you'd spend some time in my village in the Sotho Mountains. I could use a good assistant."

Happily, you agree. Never again will you feel second-rate in the company of elves.

THE END

HEART QUEST™ BOOKS

Pick a Path to Romance and Adventure™

Now! From the producers of ENDLESS QUEST™ Books

It's your first romance, and YOU must make the decisions!

#1 RING OF THE RUBY DRAGON
By Jeannie Black

#2 TALISMAN OF VALDEGARDE
By Madeleine Simon

#3 SECRET SORCERESS
By Linda Lowery

#4 ISLE OF ILLUSION
By Madeleine Simon

For a free catalog, write:
    TSR, Inc.
    P.O. Box 756, Dept. HQB
    Lake Geneva, WI 53147

TSR, Inc.
PRODUCTS OF YOUR IMAGINATION™

ENDLESS QUEST™ Books

From the producers of the DUNGEONS & DRAGONS® Game

For a free catalog, write:
  TSR, Inc.
  P.O. Box 756, Dept. EQB
  Lake Geneva, WI 53147

TSR, Inc.